MAID IN THE SHADE

Jacqueline Turner Banks

ReGeJe Press
Sacramento, California

First Edition: May 1998

10 9 8 7 6 5 4 3 2 1

This book is dedicated

To all the Sistha-girls.
To-the-bone sisthas: Clayta (my mother) and my daughter Regina.
Forever sisthas: Brenda, Carol and Carolyn; Forever sisthas part
two (the sequel) Rose, Renae, Aletha, Krystal, Darden, Dee, Rene,
Doris, Deirdre, Connie, Nyota, Cheryl and Terris. By Blood and
Marriage Sisthas: Vivian, Althea, Kimmie, Sherilynn, Luberta,
Karen, Karlene, Hija, Marcia, Lynn, Shelly, Norma and many more
just as dear. Like forever sisthas: Maggie, Pat, Geri, Ethel, Denise,
my T.T.B.O. D Sorors, and Zica (all).
My honorary sisthas: Gail, Anita, Naoma and Meg
How much? Read the back cover.

To my father and four brothers Jackson, Clayton, Spencer, Gerald
and William who made my childhood such a joy I never missed not
having a sister. And to my sons Geoffrey and Jeremy who I
wouldn't change for the world.

Always Reggie.

Juvenile novels by Jacqueline Turner Banks
(published by Houghton Mifflin)

Project Wheels
The New One
Egg Drop Blues

ONE
♠

I picked up the glass of wine and made a silent toast to me and a whole bunch of other folks: folks I don't know, but they look like me. I was feeling a bit generous so I made a toast for the many that don't look like me too, but only if they're the kind that don't mind when I get too relaxed on the cross-town bus, that's the ninety-eight, and my left leg gets heavy and flops over to the side and touches theirs just a bit. None of the people in my second toast actually had to have ridden the ninety-eight with me. They just have to be the types who won't grunt really loud in that nanosecond when our legs meet and then sigh all loud like a hungry bear and then start blowing that pastrami breath in my face. Folks that don't look like my family and don't be acting like that on the ninety-eight are all right with me. I don't worry none about what they be saying when I overhear them talking to each other, 'cause a whole lot of us Americans been raised by fools.

My Grandmama always used to say you can pick your friends, but not your relatives. And Grandmama was right too, even if she was always looking at my Mama's baby sister's husband when she said it.

And was nothing much wrong with Uncle Buddy, least that's what Daddy would say. Daddy said the only thing wrong with Buddy was he started "smelling himself too soon," and by the time (Auntie) Raylean met up with him, he was already worn out. I ain't never known what Daddy meant by that, "smelling himself too soon." It would seem to me that there's never going to be a *good* time to pick up your own scent, but that's just me talking and folks know I'm clean about myself.

I leaned back on that white sofa and sipped that wine like I knew who killed the hog. It was good too, not thick and sweet like that Mogan-David my folks used to drink on Christmas and Grandmama would sometimes put in her cake batter. The wine was just sweet enough to make my toes curl, like they do when Raymond Scott sings a solo on Sunday. But not sweet enough to make my toes curl so tight they crack—like old Raymond has been known to do during our personal Saturday night services.

And yet the wine was bitter too, if a thing can be both. The bitterness hit me right under my ears like it was trying to make them turn in on themselves. I remembered that's what Grandmama's right nipple did just before she died, but I shook off those thoughts. I don't have to think like that when I'm in a groove.

Yeah, I likes me some wine. The way I figure it, if Jesus made some out of water and passed it around, who am I to say something's wrong with it? You know what was making that wine taste even better? I'd put on an old Wes Montgomery album before I sat down. That man was in the toe curling business too. That old album was a little scratchy, but that's okay with me. There were some CDs over there, but somehow it doesn't seem right that all that pretty music can be coming out of something ain't round enough to support some fried chicken, Auntie Raylean's potato salad and some cornbread. Yes indeed, that was living. I rubbed my first finger over the mouth of that crystal wine glass and it made a humming noise. The first time I saw somebody do that I wanted to shout, "Lawd, if the wine won't talk to you the stemware will!" But I was working and I couldn't be making testimonies that some folks might deem strange. Talking strangely at the wrong time can get you locked up in a place where you can't properly dispose of your toenail clippings. I know about places like that, but I don't let myself think about it when I've got a glass of good wine and Wes Montgomery to keep me company.

I was getting ready to flip the album over and pour myself just one last taste when I heard the car in the driveway. I couldn't curse them or say "Damn" or anything, because two glasses of wine and a full side of a soulful album ain't nothing to get mad about. I took a linen napkin and wiped out my glass. The glass is part of my collection now—has been for months. I hurried and turned off the record player that they call "a system." By the time the front door opened, I was coming down the stairs with the dust mop in my hand.

"All finish upstairs?" Miz Audrey asked me.

"Yes Ma'am," I said grinning, my breath still sweet with the wine from that dusty cellar bottle.

There was something in the way she said, "welcome," that immediately pissed me off. It's not like I was running late or anything. Hell, I wonder how long it would take her to haul her fat ass off that couch and catch two buses to Miz Audrey's and back. I laughed. I could picture my "little" sister, Emerald, spread out in one of those sticky number 98 seats sitting next to the Fly Man, that's what all of us regulars call him. He's about a hundred years old and always dressed in the same dirty brown woolen three-piece suit that has big blobs of his most recent meal on his wide triangle-shaped lapels. He looks like the kind of gentleman you feel a bit sorry for. The kind of old man you figure has seen some stuff in his days, and most of it was pretty horrible. His look makes you inclined to say, "Good morning, Sir," but you better not say it. He's always looking for a smile or a little kindness from some woman, so he can sit next to her and open his fly—exposing his old withered self.

That good wine still had me buzzing. I knew my "language skills," as Miz Audrey calls them, would be worse than usual. They're always bad when I drink. I tried to pull myself together, but I got the giggles. See, what folks don't know about me, giggling just makes me giggle more—always has.

"See, Ruby, there you go again. All that strange laughing at the wrong time is what got you shackled up out at Kincaid."

"I wasn't shackled up. I coulda left at any time. Kincaid ain't nothing but a hospital, just like Mercy General. They had to restrain me for a while because I was having a bad reaction to my meds."

"And if you don't do something about your language you'll be a maid for the rest of your life. Just because those foreign nurses were out there calling them meds, doesn't mean that's what you suppose to call them."

I walked away. I work too hard to have to listen to somebody who, in a given day, doesn't move twenty feet away from her bed. Sure, she's getting disability for her bad hips, but that disability doctor wasn't in the kitchen yesterday when she made a strange move and three quarters fell out of her bra. She dived under the table like Jerry Rice trying to recover a bad pass.

I went into my tiny dining room to get my mail.

I love my little house; ain't no rental either. Every month I pay four hundred and seventy-two dollars to the bank straight out, even before I buy food. The way I figure it, both me and my sister can afford to lose a few pounds, but not nan one of us got a shell on our backs.

"Damn," I said, when I got to the dining room. "Even this room smells like her." About three months ago she ordered a perfume, no, excuse me not perfume—parfume. This parfume was supposed to capture her natural scent, therefore smelling different on every woman that wears it. Well, my sister's natural scent must be the Hudson Bay because she got the whole house smelling like rank salt water.

I gathered my mail. One good thing I can say about old Emerald, she might take a little longer than most to learn a lesson, but when she gets it, she gets it good. She finally knows I want to find my mail on the dining room table when I get home from work. I recognized Jan Channey's stationary right away. Jan Channey is the best friend I've made since being out of public school. That's saying a lot, because it's hard to make a good friend once out of school. How are you going to build trust for a person you haven't seen naked in the gym shower or haven't switched brown bag lunches with? A best friend is somebody who still respects you after you've made a fool of yourself by standing next to Floyd Connors locker every day for a whole school year. I count myself among the lucky to have Jan Channey for a best friend. And don't think we ain't that close because I use her whole name. She's one of those people who most everybody used to call by her whole name.

Jan likes to write letters. She says it's because she likes to go to her mail box and see something other than bills. You can't get letters unless you write them, everybody should know that. Jan Channey's stationary is bright red, which can be a bit confusing in December, but with it being August, I knew it was her.

I saved Jan Channey's letter to the side and thumbed through the garbage mail first; the bills and the cut off notices. I truly believe the reason so many Montgomery Wards stores are closing all over the country is because they waste so much time and money sending out so damn much junk mail. I swear, I get something in the mail from them five days outta six. I slipped off my shoes and sat. It was time to read girlfriend's letter. I could tell right away it wasn't thick enough for one of her four pagers. I opened it. It was one page long. I got my mouth ready to smile because Jan Channey can write some funny stuff.

Dear Ruby,
If you're reading this, then I'm probably already dead. If not, I'm close to it. Call my mother she'll know if I'm dead. I just wanted to tell you I love you, girl. You can do anything. Get out of that maid's uniform. I know you don't actually wear a uniform, but your mind wears one.

It was signed Love, Jan Channey. My hand was shaking when I put down the letter. Jan Channey is funny and fun; she ain't nobody's fool. She knows me well enough to know I don't be playing around with somebody being dead—I know her just as well.

After high school graduation, both of us got one year scholarships to Burns College in Maine. She came from Oakland, California and I came from Petite, Tennessee. It was a program some

11

well-meaning folk put together to get disadvantaged students ready for college. I went because it would be my first time on an airplane. I knew I didn't want to go on for a degree. Jan Channey said she came because Maine wasn't Oakland, California.

"Emerald, where's my cordless phone?"

"Not phone, Ruby, say telephone!"

"Where the hell is it?!"

"In here, next to me. And I don't know why you're getting all mad. You said you wanted to speak better. You *asked* me to help."

I went back in the living room to get it. I knew I wasn't going to find Emerald in motion bringing it to me.

TWO

♠

Dr. Audrey Gray ain't no saint. You learn some things about a person when you clean up after them. But she's got a good heart. As soon as I put down the te-le-phone, having talked to Jan Channey's mother, I called Miz Audrey.

"Miz Audrey, this here is Ruby,"

"Ruby, do you remember when you asked me to help you with your grammar?"

Well that question caught me off guard. I was the caller, clearly I had something to say and there she was taking over my conversation.

"Yes, Ma'am, I remember."

"I wish you would remember I asked you not to call me ma'am, too, we're almost the same age."

"I'm sorry."

"No, dear, don't apologize." She breathed hard like she does when she thinks I'm not getting what she's saying. "Ruby, you said this here is Ruby. All you need to say is, this is Ruby. The here part is understood."

Well she did it again. She confused me in that way of hers.

13

Was she saying she was psychic—that she already knew I was calling? What was understood? Did she understand why I was calling too? See, that's what I say about too much education, it's a dangerous thing. Miz Audrey is a doctor and all that education has made her a very confusing individual. And I don't even want to get started on those two kids of hers and her lawyer husband. My mother and a few church friends told me I was making a big mistake taking a job with black folks, but I still think they're wrong.

"She's gonna work you like a slave," Martha Ross, the organist at church told me.

But see, I know Martha's kind too. She has a desk job over at the furniture factory. She has a cleaning "crew" (two Mexican women) who come in every two weeks. I know her crew, as she likes to refer to them at every opportunity, she works *them* like slaves. Martha's kind has been around forever. My Daddy told me when he was a kid, some of the black folks in his neighborhood wouldn't buy ice from the black ice man. They claimed a block of ice from the white man lasted longer. That's just plain stupid. Martha would've been in the front of the line buying that white ice.

"Do you get what I'm saying, Ruby?"

As usual, my mind was wandering. "Yes, Ma'am, I mean Miz Audrey." I had to agree with her to get on with *my* business. Miz Audrey will make a body forget why they called if you don't just agree.

"I'm calling because of something terrible that's happening in my family."

"What is it, Ruby?"

"My half sister, Jan, is missing in Oakland. I got a letter from her today telling me she'll probably be dead when I read the letter. Her mother, I mean my ex-stepmother, is an elderly woman. I need to get out there to help her." See, I know those upper-middle class types think my kind has a bunch of half-sisters all over the place.

"Oh my God! So you're saying you need some time off?"

"No, well, yes, that too."

"Oh, you need an advance on your salary?"

"Yes, Ma'am, I mean Miz Audrey."

"Okay, let me work this out in my mind for a second."

That's Miz Audrey for you, she works things out in her mind. Sometimes I'll ask her if she wants me to change the sheets and she'll stop and work it out in her mind. The way I figure it, when a person's very educated all that education gets in the way of making fast decisions.

"Okay, Ruby. Why don't I charge your tickets and then I'll take twenty-five dollars a month out of your check until it's repaid. Does that work for you?"

"Yes, Ma'am. And I sure do appreciate it." She came to the decision I wanted her to make and I didn't even have to think it out. But I couldn't just ask her to charge a ticket for me. Folks don't need anybody telling them how to spend theirs, even I know that.

I called Raymond Scott and told him I was going to need a ride to the airport. I guess some folks would call us boyfriend and girlfriend, but at our ages there should be a better name for it. I know some people like to call their friends "lovers," but, to me that sounds nasty. When people say that, I keep expecting them to whip out some Polaroid's or something. Why else would they define their friendship by their bedroom activity?

Raymond said okay, but I knew he would. Short of work, church and me, Raymond ain't got a damn thing else to do with hisself. . . uh, himself. That's our problem, he's too set. He's good with words and money, and that old man is hell on wheels in the bedroom, but upright he bores me to death. I called him old but he's only fifty-eight, fourteen years older than me. But that's another story and Jan Channey was on my mind.

I finished with the easy part, it was time for me to go in the living room and tell Emerald. Folks think I'm dense, but if Emerald was half as smart as she thinks she is, she'd be pondering simple questions longer than Miz Audrey.

She was down on her "bad" knees, bending her "bad" hips, no doubt, looking for the TV remote.

"What'cha lose?" I asked, but like I said, I felt I knew but she could have been diving for runaway quarters again.

"You want to say, what *did* you lose? And the answer is the remote."

"Then ask and answer my next question, you swamp-smellin'.
. . ." I had to stop myself, the last thing I needed to do was piss her off
and then leave her alone in my house for a few days. Emerald has a
hoard of friends and at two hundred and fifty some-odd pounds she's
the smallest. The thought of them sitting around on my furniture, each
wearing her own special parfume, caused a shiver to run down my
back.

"Baby, wouldn't it be easier to just go over there and turn the
channel."

"What are you trying to say, Ruby? What, am I lazy or
stupid—which one?"

I swear, it hurt me to ignore a set-up like that but I did. "No,
darling, neither. I just hate to see you hurt yourself like that and I need
to talk to you."

"Will you put it on channel ten first?"

Well, I guess I knew how much attention she planned to pay
to what I had to say. I flipped the switch to channel ten and sat next
her.

"I got a letter from Jan Channey."

"I know. I recognized her red stationery. How's she doing?"

"Not good, Em." I handed her Jan's letter.

Emerald was hesitant to take the letter from me. I guess I've
been too hard on her lately; she thought it was a trick. Usually she has
to wait until I go to work to go through my stuff and read my mail.
She finally took it. She read it twice before she commented.

"Is this for real? Did you call her mother?"

I nodded.

"What she say?"

I knew Emerald left a word out of her question that she
wouldn't have hesitated to point out to me, if I'd said it, but I didn't
mention it. "She said it's true. Jan left her house on Sunday night and
she hasn't been seen since. She said her house has been shot up in
drive-bys twice in the last three weeks."

"How does she know Jan is the intended victim?"

"I asked her that too. She said that Jan had been followed

home from the BART station by a man in a white car every day last week. Jan got the feeling he was waiting for her to separate herself from the crowd, of course she didn't. Saturday night was the last time their house was shot up. Jan figured it would be safer for her family if she moved out."

"Where is she?"

"Mrs. Channey said she doesn't know."

"You say it like you don't believe her."

"I don't. That's one of the reasons I'm going out there."

"Where?"

Where? I thought she was tracking. "To California, I'm going out to Oakland."

"When?"

"Tonight, baby, as soon as Miz Audrey makes the reservations."

"What's Dr. Gray got to do with it?"

I told her about the calls I made after I talked to Jan's mom. Emerald was giving me the impression that she was really concerned and that was an unexpected warm fuzzy.

"Don't go, Ruby. Folks out there are crazy. They be killing folks and the folks don't even know why."

Again I had the grace to ignore *her* bad grammar. "Who the killers?"

"No, Girl, the dead folks don't even be knowing why they're dead! Gangs shooting up houses, perverts snatching little kids right out of their houses. And have you noticed the last few times you heard about that shaken baby syndrome it happened in California? That's a sad way to die."

She lapsed into a deep thought. I could read pain on her face. Emerald is just like all the women in my family, nothing hurts her more than a hurt baby. But surely she couldn't be worried about somebody picking up my hundred and eighty pounds and shaking me to death?

"I've got to go. You've met Jan Channey, if it was me in trouble she'd be here?"

Emerald nodded. "How can I help?"

Now that really surprised me. As close as we had been as kids, for the past two years, since she got bad hips and moved in with me, we ain't been too sisterly.

"I need you to go out and pay some bills for me. I got turnoffs on the electricity and the cable." Actually, I didn't have a turnoff on the cable and, under normal circumstances, I would have waited to pay it, but I needed her to pay the electric bill and that wouldn't mean as much to her as no cable. It wouldn't occur to her that she needed the electricity to use the cable. "Do you think you can get one of your friends to drive you?"

"Yeah, Carolyn got her car fixed. If we wait until her daughter gets out of school, she's taking summer classes, she can run in for me."

"It needs to be credited right."

"I know. Carolyn's daughters are smart. Don't worry. They take care of all of Carolyn's business. You know her back is almost as bad as my hips."

Again, I had to fight the urge to say what ran cross my mind. Ain't neither one of them, Emerald nor Carolyn, ever done enough hard work to have anything bad except their credit. And neither one of them is forty yet.

"You can count on me," Emerald said. She turned to watch the folks turning that wheel on television. I guess she'd given me all the time she had. Bless her heart. I watched the television with her for a moment, my mind mostly on which clothes to take to California. I wondered why they didn't oil that wheel. It looks to me like it's hard for some of those little California women to bend over that barrier and spin that wheel enough for it to go all the way around at least once. But the more I thought about it, I decided, I ain't never heard this man say it had to go all the way around. I was mixing him up with Bob Barker and that wheel he has folks spinning. Bob Barker can sound really bitchy telling spinners about making, "at least one rotation" with that heavy-ass wheel. Now that's a wheel that definitely needs some oil.

I went to my bedroom and stretched out on my big beautiful bed. I love my little house. See that's another thing about working for your own people. Miz Audrey has been in my house and she likes it too. She even gave me some curtains, that she already had, for my kitchen windows. She thought they would match better than the plain white ones I had up there and she was right. The woman I cleaned for before Miz Audrey brought me home one day. It was raining buckets and she said she didn't want me to get sick and not be able to work her daughter's open-house graduation party.

She decided to stop by the caterers while she was on this side of town. She asked to use my phone, this was before cellulars. I knew it was a mistake, but how do you tell the richest woman in town, who's also your boss, that she can't use the phone? She came in and immediately got that shocked look on her face that insurance men always get when they come to collect. Her face said she was expecting a dump and my house is anything but that. I worked her daughter's open house and the very next Monday she fired me. I was living too well and she didn't want to contribute to that.

Miz Audrey called and told me I could pick up my tickets at the revs (her word) counter. My flight was scheduled for an eleven seventeen departure. It was six-fifteen. I called Raymond and he said he was on his way. I was afraid he was going to say that. We're about an hour and a half from the Memphis airport. The soonest I wanted to see him was nine o'clock, maybe eight-thirty to be on the safe side.

I forced myself up. I knew if I didn't, I could fall asleep. I got my suitcase down from the closet. My Aunt Vivian gave me a good suitcase when I graduated from high school. It's the gift she gives all the nieces and nephews.

"I'm giving you this, because I want you to go somewhere and see something. Don't spend your whole life in this place."

It's the same thing she told all of us, but I was the only one to take that suitcase and go to college with it. Okay Emerald went to a business school, but it was here in town. I'm the only maid in the family too, but so what? It's an honest job and I like being self-employed. That reminded me. There was something I needed to look up in my encyclopedia. I love to read. One whole side of my bedroom is a bookcase Raymond built.

Raymond, true to his word, was ringing the doorbell while I was closing the suitcase. I ran to the door. I don't know why I ran, it wasn't like I was going to collide with Emerald.

"Hi, Sweetie," I said, hugging him. Some people would say I was kissing up, but I was feeling a little guilty about not wanting to be bothered before the trip.

"Hello, Ruby." He hugged me hard. Raymond's very physical. I'm usually the hands-off one. "What's this all about?" he asked, while moving. He was already walking in the direction of the bedroom. I had hurried and packed because I didn't want him in the bedroom. Raymond is tall, six-three, with long legs. He was already in the bedroom sitting at my vanity by the time I got in there. Miz Audrey would have said, 'let me think about that a moment,' when he asked what this was all about and he'd still be standing by the door watching her think.

Raymond never tries to stop me from doing what he knows I want to do, but that doesn't prevent him from voicing his opinion—over and over and over again. I really didn't feel like hearing it.

Against my better judgment, I sat on the bed. I told him everything. He listened with his eyes fixed on me like I was water and he was raw thirst looking to be quenched. I'm not ugly, I'm pleasantly average. I used to have a nice big juicy body and some people say my fat still stacks up well, but Raymond gives me the willies when he treats me like a precious jewel. I laughed. Ruby the jewel, I'd heard it before, I don't know why it struck me as so funny. Raymond crinkled his eyebrows together and I knew it was time to stop laughing.

Raymond called me a tease for getting him all worked up and leaving him high and dry. The operative word is dry. Old Raymond sweats like a horse when he gets going. I didn't have time to take a shower and, like I said, I like to be clean. I did think it was some awfully young-sounding talk for an old Christian man, but I didn't say anything. At eight o'clock, we were at the front door giving last minute instructions to Emerald. I was on the front steps when she opened the door and called to me.

"Ruby, the only Bart I know is that little bad ass cartoon boy. What's a Bart station?"

"Look at the encyclopedia opened on my vanity."

We were heading down I-40 when Raymond asked, "What's a Bart station?"

"Bay Area Rapid Transit, it's what they be out there calling their underwater subway."

THREE
♠

Raymond stayed with me right up until it was time to board. To his credit, he didn't try too hard to talk me out of it. He volunteered to come with me, but we both knew it was a hollow offer. Raymond works at the furniture plant, and he hasn't missed a scheduled day in ten years. I can't say it's a record that I would care about, but he's proud of it. He kissed me when the flight attendant announced the row that contained my seat. I gave him a big wet one and sent him back to Petite. I guess I love him, in my own way.

I thought about old Raymond for my first half hour in the air. He had talked to the reservation clerk about changing my ticket to a direct flight. I figured Dr. Gray got me the best possible deal, but I didn't discourage him. He thinks it's a man's job to take care of things like that. Of course there were no direct flights. The only other flight, that would have gotten me to Oakland that night, already left and had two stops, St. Louis and Las Vegas. Miz Audrey's reservation gave me enough time to get packed and my business straight and called for only one quick stop, Dallas/Ft.Worth. But I gave Raymond my ticket and let him check because good men are like that, they want to make things easier for you. I've had enough bad men to know the difference.

I wanted to sleep, but I've never been able to sleep traveling. I imagine I slept when I was a little girl riding around in my parents' big Roadmaster, but since I've been old enough to remember, I can't recall too often feeling that comfortable with the drivers I know. All around me people were sleeping with drool dripping out of their mouths, snoring, passing gas, and I was wide awake to see, hear, and smell it all.

I drive, but I haven't owned a car in two years. It died and I haven't had the money to buy another one. Raymond probably would help me get a running clunker and help me keep it running if I asked, but I really hate to ask anybody for anything,

I tried to start the novel he bought me at the airport. It was a mystery, he knows I enjoy mysteries, and I like the author's work, but I couldn't get into it yet. My mind kept returning to Jan Channey. I remembered the day we met.

Burns College is small, "a perfect little replica of a larger ivy league school." I knew that before I got there because those words were a quote from a student straight out of the catalog. By the time I got to Burns college on that Tuesday after Labor Day, I had memorized every word in the catalog. The catalog looked like it had been through a cycle in my mother's wringer washer. I read it every night before dropping off to sleep. I felt like all the cute little white kids pictured in it were my personal friends. I couldn't wait to sit at the tables in the cafeteria where the black, red and brown students from Project Bootstrap (my program, which would come to be referred to as Project BS) were sitting and laughing about what had to be the funniest thing ever said.

I remembered the hamburger that was pictured in front of one of the happy students. Never had I seen a prettier hamburger. I couldn't wait. By the time I flew into Bangor International Airport and rode the additional seventy-seven miles by bus I loved everything about this state that I couldn't remember hearing one word about until my school counselor told me about Burns.

The scenery along the way was fresh and clean. Everything looked like it had been sprayed and washed by the nearby Atlantic Ocean whose presence I felt the whole year I was there. Port Dell,

Maine, home of Burns College, wasn't a port town. The name never made sense to me, but by the time I got there I had too many more important questions to ask.

The bus dropped me off on the curb near the administration building. That's where I met Jan Channey. She was sitting on a foot locker at the top of the walkway. There was a new set of soft luggage piled around her.

"Don't tell me, Project Bootstrap, right?" she hollered, pointing at me as I struggled up the slight incline with my suitcase, a taped box, my book bag and a shopping bag. I waited until I was standing next to her before I answered. I was huffing and puffing. I wanted to be annoyed with her. There she was sitting on that footlocker, looking as cute as those kids from the catalog. I felt she could have helped, or at least saved her question until I was closer.

"Yes, I'm in Project Bootstrap," I finally answered.

"I would have helped you up the hill, but it took me three trips to get this stuff up here and I'm whipped. I'm Jan Channey, from Oakland, California. Who are you?" She was small but her voice was loud and deep, it didn't fit her body at all .

I sat on my suitcase. "I'm Ruby Gordon, from Petite Tennessee."

"Petite, Tennessee, I love it. Give it up, Girl. I know anybody from Pe-*tite*, Tennessee must have some fried chicken in one of those bags." She started laughing, a laugh even deeper than her voice.

I thought she was one of the prettiest sistha-girls I'd ever seen in real life. Her hair was cut in a medium-sized Afro. To me that in itself was remarkable. Women in my family didn't grow a whole lot of hair and the last thing we would do is have it cut and shaped in a nappy style. I could tell by the grade of her hair that growing some more wouldn't be a problem. There's an Indian man, from India, in my hometown. He's married to a white woman. They have two little girls that tan to the prettiest brown every summer. It's a combination of cinnamon, yellow, and a drop of orange. That was the color of Jan Channey's skin. Her eyes were big with long black-black lashes.

I didn't know if she was insulting me or not about that fried chicken. Actually I did have two ham sandwiches in my shopping bag. I decided to ignore her request. "What dorm are you in?" I asked.

"All of us are in Clarke. That's it." She turned around and pointed to a lovely building behind the administration building and up a steeper hill. "It's pretty, ain't it?"

I nodded.

"It looks like a cathedral, the style is federal. I'm into buildings. No," she shouted, jumping up from her footlocker. I jumped too. My first thought was that she'd been bitten by a bee. I looked around for it.

"It looks like Monticello!"

I just looked at her, surely she wasn't speaking English. I'd heard that a lot of Spanish was spoken in California.

"You know, Thomas Jefferson?"

I nodded. I did know *about* Thomas Jefferson, but I didn't know what he had to do with whatever she'd just said.

She sat back down, satisfied with herself, but Lord knows I didn't know why. She talked for the next five minutes about domes, neoclassicism architecture, and Ionic columns, most of it making little sense to me, but I was enjoying the sound and authority of her voice.

"So tell me, Ruby, what brought you to Burns College?"

I told her about it being my first airplane trip and my sleeping with the catalog and reading everything I could find about college and Maine. She laughed through most of it, but this time I found myself laughing with her.

"What about you?" I asked.

"Port Dell, Maine ain't Oakland, California—enough said?"

I could have used more, but I was willing to wait. "Why," I finally asked, "are we sitting here?"

"See those boys over there?" She pointed to two small figures pushing something too far away for me to make out what.

"I see them."

"They're bringing me a shopping cart to push my stuff up that hill."

"Wouldn't it have made more sense for them to just help you

with your luggage?"

"That's what I asked them to do, but they offered to go get the cart. What did I care, I just wanted help? I kind of got the feeling that they wanted to help me, but they didn't want to get caught up in Clarke Hall."

"Ump."

"Yeah, ump. What's up with that?"

"You think there'll be room for my stuff in there?"

"It's a fucking shopping cart, we can make anything fit. In Oakland those things are homes on wheels."

We laughed. "Jan Channey?"

"Yeah?"

"I do have a couple of ham sandwiches."

"Give it up, girl . I haven't eaten anything since this morning."

The boys finally made it to us and they were very nice about piling all of our stuff into the shopping cart. It was heavy, all four of us took turns pushing it separately and together up the hill.

"Okay, now you'll need to push it over to the desk and get your room numbers, they'll be on the right side. All of the dorms have the girls on the right. After you unload it, just leave it out here. We'll get it later," the shortest, cutest boy said. I think I remember the other one calling him Jim, but they never introduced themselves.

"Won't somebody rip it off?" Jan Channey asked. It was nineteen seventy and that was the first time I'd ever heard the expression "rip off." I could guess what she meant, but I was sure the white boys wouldn't know.

They gave each other knowing looks. "Stealing is not a problem at Burns," the tall one said.

"Cool," Jan answered, flashing them one of her soon-to-be-famous Jan Channey flirty smiles.

"Anyway," the shorter one spoke. "It doesn't belong to us. It'll get pushed around campus today and tomorrow and work its way back over to our frat house."

We thanked them and went into the building. I was surprised when Jan Channey said, "I thought for sure the little cute one was going to try to hit on me." She said it very casually, like white boys hitting on her was an everyday thing. I had to remind myself that she was from California. Or, maybe more importantly, Jan wasn't from Petite, Tennessee.

The dorm was just as beautiful as it looked from outside. Jan spent the first few moments looking up at the ceiling, its exposed beams and columns, and pointing out various details to me. The older student, at what looked like a hotel check-in counter, was friendly. She told Jan Channey she was in room 202 and I was in 198.

"You two are wall mates."

"Can we be roommates?" Jan asked.

The student looked around. "I'm not supposed to do this." She pulled a packet of cards out of slot 198 and switched it with a packet in slot 202. "The keys and everything are in the packets. Your RA, that means Resident Assistant, should be in sometime today to introduce herself and answer any questions. They're all over at the welcome ceremony now."

"Should we be there?" Jan asked.

The girl's cheeks colored. "No, most of the Bootstrap students don't come up with their parents. The ceremony is kind of designed for the parents. Trust me, you aren't missing anything."

"We trust you," Jan Channey said, grinning and immediately putting the girl at ease.

As soon as we walked away Jan asked, "so, we'll put this shit away and then go crash their welcome ceremony?"

"Are you serious?"

"Absolutely."

We pushed the cart to the elevator. When we got to our room, we dropped everything in the middle of the floor. Outside, Jan asked the first girl we saw where were they holding the welcome ceremony. The girl said she hadn't heard anything about it. She was black, actually Afro-American back then. We passed two more black girls before Jan asked again, this time a white girl.

"Last year it was in Washington Hall. That's the building closest to us." Again, like the others, she was very friendly. I would have thought the administration building was the closest, but I was wrong. Directly behind Clarke Hall was a round-shaped building. We crashed the ceremony and ate some great snacks. Jan taught me that the cute little cakes were called petite fours. She taught me another new word. We "tripped" as we watched teens and their parents crying their goodbyes, acting like somebody had died. It was the beginning of a friendship that was approaching three decades.

I closed the book and stopped pretending I was reading. I closed my eyes, sure I couldn't sleep, but trying anyway.

My eyes were still closed when I heard the pilot say we were making our approach to the Oakland airport. He said the time was eleven-thirty and the temperature was sixty-seven degrees. The information surprised me. I was shocked we were in California. I must have fallen sho-nuff asleep to have missed the Dallas stop. Until the pilot said it, I'd forgotten about the time change and I expected California to be warmer.

FOUR
♠

I'd heard so much about Oakland, California, from Jan, that I probably had an image in my head that would have been impossible to meet. I was immediately disappointed by the airport. It wasn't as "big city" as Memphis's. I clutched my purse as I eased down the aisle, sure a sunshine-loving home boy would meet me at the gate ready to wish me a happy day and grab my purse, two hundred in cash and all.

"Enjoy your stay in Oakland," the fancy-faced flight attendant told me, as I exited. I clutched my bag a little tighter. Between Jan, and the west coast "Oaktown" rappers on the station Emerald listens to, fear was causing my heart to race. The nervous attack caught me by surprise. I'm not usually the scary type. I'm a big woman who's fought off my share of creeps. Neither my back nor hips are bad. But the rules have changed since I was a young woman. Kids that used to give women my age a mouthful of lip, nowadays are subject to have a clearly visible uzi. I can't fight this new fight but I'm just as inclined to try and that's the problem. I can still give face like a tough woman but my heart is out to make me a liar.

I stepped into the brightly lit airport my nerves calmed. It was as clean as any public building I've ever entered. Everything looked new. It was late, almost midnight, and not many people were about. The only rowdiness I could hear or see was coming from the passengers from my flight complaining about California's strict no smoking laws. I don't believe in taking rights and privileges from folks, but there's something to be said about the clean that comes with smokeless. I walked with the crowd to baggage claim. There was a sense of smallness to the building. It had everything the Memphis airport had but less of it or maybe reduced sizes of it. I've been in homes like that. Houses with just as many rooms as Miz Audrey's big house but somehow the feel was small. Like the rooms were compact versions of a home large enough to need a cleaning woman. The bags came in pretty fast and within minutes I was out front looking for a taxicab. I probably don't have the same problems black men have getting a taxicab but I've had my share of grief. I was planning to go downtown and get a room and then strike out in the morning to Jan's mother's house, but it wasn't going to be that easy. The first two drivers I approached told me they didn't go downtown. One of them wouldn't even look at me. He just mumbled the words out of the side of his mouth. I knew that was a lie. What taxicab driver in any major city doesn't go from the airport to downtown? I figured they either thought I was lying and using downtown as a way of saying "take me to the ghetto." Or maybe they thought I wanted to rob them. I guess it happens, but it pissed me off to have to suffer for something I would never do. I'm sure some of them have been robbed by white men, but has it stopped them from picking up white people? I remembered a conversation I had with Miz Audrey about something similar.

"That's the nature of being a minority You're held responsible for all the bad things done by the group. Wait a minute let me think about that." She paused and put on her thinking face. "You know, Ruby, sometimes it works the other way too. Do you remember my friend, Dr. Wong?" I nodded "She says other doctors are always coming up to her to work out math problems like how many milligrams of a drug for a certain weight." Miz Audrey laughed. "Her math is terrible but they expect her to be a math whiz because she's Asian."

That why I like being around Miz Audrey I'm always learning something. I didn't know Asians were supposed to be math whizzes. And I like the way Miz Audrey makes me feel like I'm teaching her things too. Like one day I told her Matthew, her little boy, was probably coming down with something. When she asked me how did I know. I told her his pee was a deep yellow and my mother always said she could tell when baby boy had fever because of the color in his diapers. Matthew did come down with some kind of feverish cold. About a month later she told me she checked with some of the nurses who worked with babies and they confirmed (her word) that the feverish baby boys usually had deep yellow pee.

I looked around and spotted the stand for the hotel vans. I read the writing on the outside of each of them. None of them seemed to be from downtown hotels. I changed my plan and decided to spend the night at an airport hotel; surely taxi drivers would be friendly in the day light. Last year I got one of those secured credit cards. My income wasn't big enough to get a regular bank card. I had to deposit three hundred dollars in a savings account and I got a four hundred and fifty dollar credit limit. I hadn't used it yet, mainly because the interest is so high, but I loved the idea of having one to charge my room. It had been hard not telling Emerald about it. But I knew she would have found some desperate reason to charge something before now.

I walked over to the prettiest van. "Are there any vacancies at the Coaster?" I asked the driver.

"I'm sure there are."

He got out and helped me with my bag. He was a Mexican. I tried to remember the word Miz Audrey told me to use. Hispanic, he was Hispanic.

"So, Sister, are you out here on business?"

I did a double-take. No, he wasn't any kind of black man I was used to seeing. I didn't have a problem being his sister, I just wasn't expecting it.

"I'm kind of surprised it's so cool."

He laughed. "Yup, people always say that. When I worked at the Peninsula Coaster, it's across the bay where it's even colder, people would get mad at me about the night weather. Where're you from?"

"Near Memphis."

"Yeah, you've got humidity down there. It holds the heat. When the sun goes down here, the heat goes with it. But if you stay on this side it should be warm enough for you during the day."

We were sitting in the van. I was starting to really relax now. Not knowing where I was going to spend the night had me a little jittery, but that ain't me admitting to an anxiety attack.

"I'm waiting for one more passenger. Here he comes now."

A middle-aged white man in a business suit was walking toward the van. The driver slipped on a cap the same bright red as the van and jumped down to the curb

"Mr. Oldenberg, good to see you."

"Hello, Jose. Where's your A's cap?"

"They make me wear this now. It's cool, this is their time not mine."

"That's the attitude. You wouldn't see me here once a month if it was my choice."

"I heard that."

I had moved over but the business man sat next to Jose. He jumped when he saw me. "Oh, we have company tonight."

Jose put on his seat belt. "Yes, we got a little class in the van tonight."

That was nice. I smiled at him in the mirror, but I don't think he saw it. He was already talking to his passenger about baseball

"I'll need to rent a car tomorrow and drive over to San Francisco," the man said. The two of them started talking about San Francisco like it was the worst hell hole the devil ever spit out. I had to interrupt.

"I've always heard great things about San Francisco," I said.

"Yeah they spend more on tourism," Jose said.

The man laughed. "Good point, Jose, those business classes are really paying off, aren't they? He's right, Miss. San Francisco is just another city except it has a lot of hills and silly pastel colored houses." They both laughed.

32

"If you decide to go over there, take a jacket," Jose advised.

We were pulling up to the Coaster. It wasn't as big as some of the other hotels we'd passed, but I could tell from the outside it was elegant. This was going to be my third time in a hotel and my first time alone. I was as excited as a kid at Disney World.

There was no hassle at the check-in counter, always a cause for joy to folks of my hue. She took my credit card without checking my ID or a print out sheet of bad cards or a quick call to some 800 number. She called me Miss Gordon and beckoned for a young guy to take my bags to my room. I know about tips, I took out two dollars and handed it to him

My room was huge. There were two queen-sized beds, a desk, and a little round oak wood table with two chairs. And it had a balcony that overlooked the pool. It was painted a dusty rose and the bed spreads had flowers in them the color of the room. There were matching paintings above each bed that also picked up the dusty rose of the walls. I spent the first ten minutes jumping from bed to bed. I wondered what the people the floor under me were thinking. Finally, I got my fill of playing. I showered, changed into a silky nightgown I've been saving for something special, and floated around the room talking to an imaginary gentleman caller.

I tried not to think about whatever the next day had to offer. I tried to hold back the thought of my friend being dead. I was Miss Gordon in room 226 of the Oakland Airport Coaster Inn and that ain't nothing to be sad about.

FIVE

♠

The seven o'clock wake up call frightened me. Phone calls when I'm sleep mean somebody's dead, that's the way it's always been. When Grandma finally, mercifully, died, Mama called at five o'clock; it was still dark outside and all.

"Roo-bee," she whined. I knew somebody was dead. I just wanted her to tell me who. Grandmama was the likely candidate, she was the sickest, but we all know the stories about the care givers being the ones who drop dead before the sick ones. Aunt Raylean and Aunt Vivian were the ones running back and forth to the hospital, feeding Grandmama, making sure the nurses gave her pain medication as often as the doctor ordered, and keeping her clean

"Oh Roo-ooo-bee," she said again.

"It's okay, Mama, just tell me who?"

"Who what?"

"Who died? Who died, Mama?" I was trying to be calm.

"My Mama Roo-bee."

She said it like I was an idiot. It didn't seem to be the time to tell her about my theory about the care-givers dropping off first. I went to my mother like she knew I would. I took care of her and I handled Grandmama's business. And when it was all over and she

34

didn't need my help anymore she started back in, bugging me about being a maid. She even bought me a fancy leather briefcase for my birthday that month. That ain't no kind of gift for a maid—that's criticism.

I picked up the telephone. "This is the front desk Miss Gordon it's seven o three."

"Thank you." I knew about tipping but maybe not everything I needed to know. Was I supposed to tell her, "I'll tip you later?"

I wanted to roll over, which surprised me because my body should have been feeling like 9:03. It was bright out, sunny. I don't know why I was expecting clouds. Maybe it had something to do with LA smog. I do know I loved the feeling of waking up in a clean room that I hadn't and wouldn't clean. I could've spent a few hours reading, maybe even ordering room service, but I know those kind of days will probably have to come in my next life. The only life I needed to be thinking about was Jan's.

I'd told Jan's mother I was coming, but I don't think she believed me. It was time to call.

I found I was a little stiff getting out of bed to get my address book from my purse. I told myself it was the long plane ride and the air-conditioned room, but what's my excuse for the recent other mornings? It's been happening a lot lately.

"Good morning, Mrs. Channey?"

"Who?" she asked

I shouted. "Good morning, Mrs. Channey"

"Yes," she shouted back. "This is Mrs. Channey."

When we were roommates twenty years ago, Mrs. Channey called Jan every first Sunday. Jan supposed her mother had somehow got a mind-set to connect checking on her with communion Sunday at church. Her telephone conversations were lively, they always left Jan in the mood for mischief. Whenever I'd answer the phone, she'd say, "How's my Tennessee Baby?" We would chat for a few minutes. The past two days I'd spoken to a woman only faintly similar to the old Mrs. Channey. I think she's losing her hearing and already missing some of her mind

"This is Ruby." I listened. "Ruby your Tennessee baby!"

35

"Lord have mercy. It sure enough is. How's my girl?"

"I'm fine, Mrs. Channey. I'm in Oakland."

"No baby she ain't in Oakland. Wasn't that you I talked to yesterday?"

I held the receiver away. Her voice was starting to ring in my ears "I'm at the Oakland airport!"

"You're at the airport?"

"Yes Ma'am."

"You coming out?"

"I'm here. In Oakland. I'm at the Coaster's Inn."

There was a pause. I could picture her thinking out my words. She didn't say she needed a moment to think about it but it was the same as with Miz Audrey. Thinking stuff through. I promised myself I would start right then and there.

"In Oakland. Lord have mercy. My little Tennessee Baby. Come on over and see me. I ain't got no car but my son-in-law does, he'll be home at three."

"No Ma'am. I'm really comfortable taking the bus."

"The bus?"

"The bus." I said a little louder.

"No, I don't know how to get here on the bus. Just ask one of the maids. They've probably got some colored maids around there that come out from Oakland. Tell them you want to get to the west side."

"Yes Ma'am."

She spent the next few minutes telling me her street address and updating me on Jan. She was claiming still not to have seen her but I still felt she wasn't telling me everything.

I choose a pair of jeans and a lightweight knit top to wear. The top was new made out of an African design print. Very casual, very California, or so I thought. I'd been tempted to take another shower. They had one of those massage attachments and last night had been fun.

With one final glance around the room, I dragged myself out. I could've stayed a week, it would have been all the vacation I wanted.

When I got to the check-out counter, I found Jose standing there talking to a young woman. He looked different in the daylight and I would have passed him by if he hadn't spoken first.

"Hey, Tennessee, good morning. Is it warm enough for you today?" He really looked different, taller and a little darker. But there was only one person in Oakland who could greet me that way. I was reminded again of the first time I met Jan Channey. He was open and cheerful like she'd been.

"Actually it's a little cool in here I haven't been out yet." I'd thought about what I was going to say and was able to eliminate what I would have said, 'I ain't been out yet.' Yes, there was something to this thinking before talking stuff.

"It's a nice day. It should get up to about eighty."

I didn't know how to check out but I've been raised to face things head-on. I slid my key across the counter to the girl. Jose was grinning at her, looking like he could lap the youth dew off her face. She was cute and as racially unclear as Jose. Her teeth needed some work and that kind of thing is important to me, but I wasn't in the market for a young girl or any other kind of woman. But that ain't me judging them that are. The way I figure it, God made all of us and he or she doesn't make any mistakes.

"I'm checking out," I said, like I say it every Friday morning in hotels across the country. I stole a glance at Jose and found some nap in his hair right around his ears. A second shot told me it might have been chemically straightened. I looked at hers. Whatever he was, she wasn't the same. Her hair was naturally curly but long and thick enough to make it fall kinda straight to her shoulders.

"Did you enjoy your stay?"

"Sure did. Thank you."

I expected her to ask for my credit card, but I remembered the night person had already seen it. Maybe I wanted the opportunity to whip it out again.

"So are you off to see the city?" Jose asked, as I signed a paper that was charging me a dollar twenty-five for my local call to Jan's mother

"I won't have a lot of time for sightseein'—sightseeing. In

fact, maybe you can help me. I need to take the bus to West Oakland."

"How far west? I have a class this afternoon I'm going that way."

I showed him the paper with Mrs. Channey's address on it

"Oh yeah, I know exactly where this is. It's in the hood. I'll drop you off."

"I don't want to be a bother." I wasn't quite sure if he was saying he would drop me off in the hotel van and charge me or if he was saying he would drop me off as a favor.

"No problem I'm going that way"

"Yeah, let him take you. Otherwise he'll stand around here all morning and get me fired."

"Don't flatter yourself, Angel."

I didn't know what that was all about, but it was young folks business and I had a chance to stay out of it.

"I need to call you something other than Tennessee if you're going to ride in the Babemobile."

"Ha," the counter-girl said.

"I'm Ruby Gordon from Petite, Tennessee."

They both laughed. I think my accent might have been particularly thick just then. I wasn't offended it happens all the time when I'm out of the south

"Well, Ruby, let's book." Jose said.

Now I try to keep up with my slang, but I wasn't quite sure what booking involved. He started walking so I followed, if it required more than that I'd have to be tardy until somebody told me differently.

"I'm parked in the employee's lot."

I don't know why he told me that except maybe it was one of those awkward moments when somebody had to say something.

"You work mornings too?" I was trying to make conversation. Surely if he had to work, we wouldn't be walking toward the employee's lot with each of us awfully aware of the strangeness of the other.

"No I just came to pick up my check. I'm off until Tuesday.

This is my three-day weekend."

We went through a heavy gray metal door that opened up to a parking lot. It was shockingly bright outside. I wished I had thought to bring my sunglasses. I saw him take a small black banana shaped plastic box with three keys hanging from it out of his pocket. I assumed it was a key chain, but it was big enough to have second purpose too. He held it up like one of those phasors Emerald's Star Trek characters are always pointing at each other. He pushed it and I heard a beep, but I wasn't able to tell where it came from

"I'm this blue CRX here."

I didn't know what a CRX was, but luckily there was only one blue car nearby. I thought I'd made a mistake until I figured out that he was opening the passenger side door for me. Raymond does that too, but I wasn't expecting it from one so young. He put my luggage in the back seat although small as the back was I was glad I only had one bag.

"So you're trying to date the girl at the counter?" I asked, once we were both inside.

"Not really. She was trying to clown on me in there. It's more like she's trying to get with me. I had to stop wearing my beeper to work, she was beeping me so much. But I ain't got time for all of that."

"All of what?"

"Angel's trying to find a husband. She made the mistake of letting me overhear her talking to one of the other girls. She's got a sweet little daughter and an apartment she's paying too much for. I ain't trying to hear none of that."

It seemed the more we moved from the hotel the more he sounded like a brother. I can understand. We all have our work vocabularies and our comfortable words.

"Where are you from?" I asked

"Oaktown born and raised."

"Oh."

He laughed. "Or were you asking what am I?"

I felt heat rise to my face. "I guess I was. I didn't mean no offense."

"None taken. I get a lot of that from out-of-state visitors. People here almost never ask."

"Why is that?"

"We're all mixed up out here. You'll see, after you spend more time out here. The girl at the counter, Angel, is part Hawaiian and Chinese on her mother's side and Hispanic on her father's side."

That was all very interesting but not getting me any closer to the answer.

"Both of my parents were born in Puerto Rico. My mother is half white, half black. My father believes most of his relatives were of African and Indian descent. And no, you can't try out your Spanish on me. I don't speak it."

"Are you kidding? I have a hard enough time with English."

We both laughed We were on a freeway as busy as any Interstate through Memphis

"So do you consider yourself Black?"

"Absolutely. And it doesn't matter what I consider myself. People look at me and they see Black, that's all that matters."

I nodded. He was right. I made a mental note to look up Puerto Rico in my encyclopedias. Buying two every other week at the grocery store was really paying off.

"But what you'll see here in California is what the country is going to look like in the next two decades."

"Yeah, you're probably right."

"From the sadness in your voice, I take it you're another one of those sisters that'll give a brother a hard time about . . . "

"About sleeping with the enemy? Yeah, I didn't know there was a group of us, but I take some offense. We've been as brainwashed as you all and yet most of us are opting to be alone if we can't have a brother-man."

"For the record, I believe the darker the berry the sweeter the juice."

We drove a few minutes in silence. I think the conversation had become too personal, too quickly. We needed a cooling-off period.

"Where are we?" I finally asked, when the silence became

weird.

"A lot of us natives still call this the Nemitz freeway, but it's the 880. That's the Coliseum over there."

I nodded. I knew about the Roman Coliseum. Jan used to talk about its design. I figured this one off of this freeway in Oakland, California probably had something to do with sports; a subject I couldn't care less about. I tried to get a feel for some of the neighborhoods we were zipping by, but Jose was driving too fast. Everybody was driving too fast for my taste. It reminded me of the time Raymond and I went to Chicago for a church conference. Chicago, now there lives some fast driving fools. One thing did jump out at me.

"Jose do all the garages be out in the front like that?" I spoke before I thought. Miz Audrey told me about putting all those unnecessary "be(s)" in my comments. I could see him thinking about my question. I was thinking it probably didn't sound like English to him.

"That's a good question. Now that I think about it, I can't think of one home I know that has the garage in the back or on the side. It's different back east isn't it?"

"I don't know about the east, but it ain't—isn't garage front in the south."

"Out here we call everything back east, except Oregon and Washington and we call them up north."

I noticed we were getting off the freeway. His street driving wasn't quite as fast.

"Are we nearby?" I asked.

"Soon. I wanted to show you my favorite place in Oakland first."

My heart jumped. Up until he said that I'd forgotten all about being in the car with a stranger. He'd stopped seeming like a stranger. I'm afraid I was thinking of him as Jan's little brother or somebody I would consider as harmless. Not thinking things out again got me in this, I told myself. I wasn't going to slip up again. I wondered if he could hear my heart.

"Where is that?" I asked, trying to be cool, trying to do some

41

serious recovery thinking. He was moving too fast for me to jump out. He wasn't as big as me, but he was buffed (Emerald's word). I couldn't take him, but maybe I could slow him down and make enough noise to get some help. What was it I heard on Oprah? Don't cry help, cry fire, loud, and as often as you can.

"It's the lake. Lake Merritt. Isn't it great?"

We were pulling into a parking space in front of, like he said, a damn lake.

There were runners and people that looked like students and retirees all around us. We were out in the open and he'd been lucky to get a parking space where we did.

"I come here all the time. Sometimes I'm too-hyped to sleep when my shift is over, so I come over here and look at the moon reflecting off the water. The police are cool about it too. I don't get hassled that often."

I was breathing easier. If he wanted to stop and look at some water who was I to complain? If it got to be too long, I would just leave and take a bus the rest of the way. I had to be closer to Mrs. Channey's, maybe I could take a taxi.

"You'd think with the ocean and bay so close I couldn't get too excited about this little lake. But I like being around people and I feel lonely on the beaches."

"I guess a lot of people in California are probably water lovers. Personally, I don't want to see more than I can find in a bathtub."

He didn't take his eyes off the water while he laughed.

"So tell me Ruby Gordon, from Tennessee, what brings you to Oakland?"

I truly hadn't planned to tell him about Jan Channey. I must have been feeling guilty about planning to beat his ass as hard as God would've allowed.

"Wow that's deep," he said when I finished.

"Yeah, I guess it is."

"What makes you think her mother knows something?"

"Just a feeling, but I trust my feelings."

He reached over me to his glove box. "Here's one of my

cards. Call me if you need a ride somewhere or some help. I don't have a damn thing to do today after my class."

I took the card. "This is so nice of you."

"You remind me of somebody."

"Who? "

"Just somebody I used to know."

I stole a glance at Jose. Some big ole brown-skinned sister must have broken the boy's heart. I could see it in his eyes. We talked for about another twenty minutes before he looked at his car clock and decided it was time to get to his class.

He was one of the most mannered young men I've been around in years. He had home-training like a southern boy, actually like southern boys used to get.

I was waving goodby to him from Mrs. Channey's steps when I finally decided to look at his card and put it in my purse. It was a plain white card with the name Jose Montero. He had a phone number message and beeper number listed. It didn't have any kind of little sign in the corner or a job title. I guess people be out in California getting business cards even when they don't have a business. The thought of getting a card: Ruby Gordon Professional Maid, crossed my mind and I knew it was something I would actually do as soon as I could. I've only got one phone number, but I do have a business of my own.

SIX
♠

Mrs. Channey's house was yellow or some color between beige and yellow. The garage was right out front, flush with the front door. I could tell it was going to be small inside. All of the houses on her street looked small. It was before noon on a Friday, but I could see enough big wheels, toys, and worn-out grass in some of the yards to know that the quiet I was hearing probably would be gone soon after three o'clock. Two maybe three of the homes on the block were very well-maintained, good paint jobs and green lawns. One or two needed paint and had no lawn. The rest were somewhere between. Mrs. Channey's was between, leaning toward the bottom. Her doorbell was hanging out by two wires. I knocked hard. I could hear the television. Folks in San Francisco should have heard her television. I knocked again, this time on her large picture window.

"Comin'," she sang out. The television volume dropped by about half to almost normal. She opened the door looked at me and then my suitcase. The thought that ran through her mind didn't compute; I could see confusion on her face.

"Yes?" she asked.

"It's me, Ruby, Mrs. Channey," I shouted. She jerked back like my loudness had struck her. Again I could almost see the little wheels turning. Ruby luggage, Ruby luggage.

"My Tennessee baby! Girl, get yoself in here!" She tried to hug me and make a grab at my suitcase in the same move. The only thing she accomplished was bumping me in the mouth with her bluish-tinted hair.

"I'm sorry, Baby." She rubbed my mouth and I smelled onions on her fingertips.

"Let me get the suitcase Mrs. Channey." I didn't wait for her to answer. I gave her a quick peck on the cheek and grabbed the suitcase.

"It's kind of stuffy in here. I'll open the door."
She left the door open and latched the screen, such as it was. There were two big holes in it, both fist size. One was at my eye level the other one about waist high. I knew I couldn't sit facing that screen. I would become too fixed on watching the comings and goings of flies.

"Child, I believe you look exactly the same as the last time I saw you. Let me see, that was 19 and 75 wasn't it, at Jan's graduation?"

"Yes, ma'am." I knew I didn't look like a twenty-something year old, if I had she would have recognized me.

"Sit down, sit down. Girl, you're at home now."

I sat in the easy chair that I figured wasn't hers. Both were covered in that ugly brocade that old black women think rich white women buy. Both were evenly dirty at an acceptable level, but the other one was worn down more and facing both the front door and the television. It had to be her chair

"I'm going to get you something to drink, don't try to stop me." She talked standing over me from behind. There was a lace doily on the back of the chair. I thought she was smoothing it out when she moved quickly to whisper in my ear, "we can't talk here. Just play along."

It happened so fast and was so unexpected I thought I imagined it. I didn't think she could move that fast or be that clever. Jan used to say her mother had her own bag of tricks which was an approved way to call someone clever back then, but the woman I'd talked to the past two days was mixing ammonia and bleach.

"As thirsty as I am, I wouldn't fight with you about something to drink."

I looked at her as she walked to the kitchen. She was moving slowly again. Humming a tune that I knew was religious, but I couldn't name. I looked around the little house. It was clean, not as clean as I could get it, but as clean as it needed to be. It surprised me that there weren't any pictures on the oak wood entertainment center. I have a picture of Jan Channey standing in front of it and I recalled framed pictures all over the shelves.

Some poor soul was crying on the soap opera Mrs. Channey had been watching. The television looked days new. That's when it hit me— the drive-bys. Whoever shot up the house must have hit the old television and the framed pictures. I looked down at the worn carpet for glass. I know it's almost impossible to get every sliver of glass out of a carpet until it's been vacuumed a couple of times. I got up and walked over to the dining area. I bent down. By leaning to an angle I could see the glittering effects of the sun bouncing off of fine glass pieces. I hurried back to my chair. I doubt if she would have minded me looking, but clearly she didn't want to talk about it yet.

Mrs. Channey returned carrying two tall glasses filled to the top with a dark liquid that looked like cola.

"Let's step out back. I'll show you my yard," she offered.

I stood and reached for one of the glasses. I was a little surprised when she said, "No, this one," and handed me the glass she wanted me to have. She started walking back in the direction of the kitchen and I followed.

Her kitchen was small and clean. There was a pot simmering on the stove. The only kitchen smell I recognized was onions. She opened a heavy wooden door and we stepped out into the bright sunlight.

I guess I shouldn't have expected much of a yard except that she *had* offered to show it. There wasn't anything about her yard that should have been a source of pride. There was a worn wood plank fence about ten feet in front of us. The yard had probably been all playground quality grass at one time. Now it was patches of grass, weed and dirt in a pattern that didn't seem to indicate normal wear from overuse. It was dead and dying from neglect.

"Jan told me not to talk to you in the house. I don't know if she thinks somebody has the house wired or what?"

I had to hold back a smile. I didn't know what was going on, but I was pretty sure it didn't involve anybody sophisticated enough to "wire" her house. Jan was probably telling her mother not to talk around people in the house.

"Do you live alone Mrs. Channey?"

"No, I've got a grandson living with me and my youngest daughter and her husband and, of course, Jan when she gets back."

It didn't seem like the little house would hold that many people, but I'm no stranger to how many folks you can cram into one house—especially if somebody else is coming in to clean up after them. I thought about a family I worked for one month and got a bad taste in my mouth.

"I have a number for you to call. I'm not sure where it is, but it's area code 415 so it's across the bay. She wouldn't tell me where she staying, but I think I know."

"Tell me exactly what's happening Mrs. Channey." I was beginning to feel like I'd walked into the middle of a movie. Maybe there was something she thought I knew that needed to be said.

"What do you mean?"

"I don't understand what's happening."

She took a long sip from her glass and for the first time I smelled the alcohol in it.

"How's anybody gonna understand all this craziness, child?"

"Can you tell me what happened when you first knew something was wrong?"

"Let's go over here and sit. I can't stand that long anymore." She led me to the side of the house. There was a weather-worn pine park bench which had seen better days.

"Sit on it, but don't scoot. You could end up with an ass full of splinters."

I rubbed the surface of the spot I planned to sit on. Didn't anything jump up to bite me. I sat down and sipped my cola. It was nice and cold, but I didn't see any ice cubes in it. It was kind of slushy like she had taken it from the freezer.

"Okay, see, about two years ago . . . "

Oh hell, I thought, any story that starts off like that is going to run longer than my attention span. She talked about how a neighbor gang called the Shivs was trying to recruit Rasan, Jan's then fourteen year old son. The leader, a youngster named Medicine Man, was hell-bent on making him a member.

"That boy tried everything. I thought there was something unnatural about it. I watch the talk shows, you know what I mean?"

I wasn't quite sure what she meant, but I figured she was either saying the boy was sexually attracted to Rasan or obsessed on some other level. I watch talk shows too.

"Finally Rasan convinced them that he wasn't disrespecting the gang, but he was an athlete and he just didn't have the time to hang out. He has a goal, to play college ball. I don't know how much you know about gangs, but they'll leave the athletes alone."

"I didn't know that."

"Yeah, they know sports take a full commitment and they don't really want anybody in who can't love the gang more than anything else. And sports is one of the few things they respect. Plus they'll help a neighborhood athlete. They bought Rasan two pairs of good basketball shoes and a couple of pairs of sweats. I guess you can say they adopted him. When he got to high school, they started coming to his home games. My friend, Betty, has a daughter who's a cop. She works with gangs and she told me ain't nothing unusual about that. Anyway that was two years ago We figured it was all over but then the harassment started again."

"How do you know it's the gang?"

"See that's the thing, we don't know. Rasan is living with his other grandparents. They live about seven blocks over." She pointed like I could see the house if I'd just look. "He asked Medicine Man why they're hassling his family again."

"What'd he say?"

"He denied being involved. He thought maybe one of the other gangs were trying to get to the Shivs by messing with Rasan.

Rasan is six-four now. He's playing varsity basketball. Medicine Man claims to be proud of my grandson. He said they want to know who's messing with him. He told Jan they would take care of it if she gives them a name."

I couldn't imagine Rasan being that tall. Jan Channey met me in Las Vegas one year. I couldn't remember the exact year, but I do remember her telling me that she decided to bring him because she didn't have to pay for a child under two. It was the last time I saw him. I was thinking about that to keep from thinking about how Medicine Man and his boys would take care of it.

"Jan figures either Medicine Man is lying or another gang is after us or somebody is trying to make it look like one of the two. You should have been here when she figured it out. You know how she is with numbers?"

I nodded. Jan Channey was another one of those mathematical geniuses that the ghetto tends to produce that mainstream America never learns about.

"Girl," Mrs. Channey started laughing, like remembering really tickled her. I noticed her glass was empty and decided to take a sip of mine. "She gave everybody involved a number then she figured it out like it was a math problem. My child sho has a head on her shoulders, doesn't she?"

"Ma'am?"

"You're going to help her so she doesn't get it blown off her little shoulders?"

"Yes Ma'am."

"I've got her number written down in the house. You can walk around to the liquor store to call."

"Write down Medicine Man's number and address too."

She had been in the process of standing. She froze for a moment and looked at me. I thought her back had slipped out, something Emerald's knees tend to do when I ask her to help me clean the house. I jumped up to help her to a full stand.

"I'm okay, baby, I stopped because you said something foolish."

"I did, what?"

"You don't talk to Medicine Man. The best you can hope for is to put the word out that you'd like him to contact you, and since he doesn't know you, he won't. But you don't just dial him up like you would a normal man."

"Why not? Isn't this just some kid we're talking about? How old is he?"

"He's about twenty, but that's like dog years if you've been in a gang for four years and the leader for two of them. No, you leave Medicine Man to Jan. They got report? Is that the word she used?"

"Rapport."

"Yeah, that's what they got."

We started back around to the backside of the house. I felt a presence before I saw him. When we got to the screen door, a man was there. He was standing perfectly still.

"I thought you were out there talking to yourself, Grandma." His voice was young and cheerful, but his eyes were cold and fixed right on me, staring like he was convinced I was the one who offered his grandmother the first drink she ever took.

"No, baby. I'm out here visiting with one of your aunt Jan's oldest friends." She looked at me, and I believe my name slipped her mind for a moment. "Ruby, this is Glenn, he's my son Luther's only child."

I remembered that Luther was the brother Jan lost in Vietnam. He was already dead when I met her; which meant this boy was older than he looked and Luther must have started a family very young. He was nineteen when he died.

"Pleased to meet you."

But he damn sure didn't look pleased to meet me. I followed Mrs. Channey back into the kitchen. She stopped at the refrigerator's freezer and took a two-liter bottle of Coke out. She poured about two inches in her glass. She then went to a cabinet and got a bottle of Bicardi's rum and filled the glass the rest of the way. I looked at her, if she had drunk that much the first time, I was expecting her to fall flat on her face at any moment. But when she started walking toward the living room her gait was as straight and careful as it had been from the jump.

Just before sitting in her chair, I noticed she glanced at a small travel alarm clock in one corner of the entertainment center. "Turn to channel four for me," she told her grandson, who had followed us into the room. Another soap opera had already started. She positioned herself in a way that told me this was one she planned to watch. Her grandson stood behind her chair, still not attempting to hide his curiosity about me.

"You staying here?" he asked, his voice gruff, but not completely unkind.

"Of course she is. Take her suitcase to my room." I didn't think Mrs. Channey was paying much attention, but apparently she was.

"Why don't you come and see where it is? Grandma is going to be zoned-out for the next forty-five minutes."

He wasn't looking at me, but it didn't take a genius to know I had to be the person he was talking to.

"Excuse me, Ruby. He's right this is my favorite show. Let him show you where you're going to be, if you don't mind sharing a bed with an old lady." She laughed. I thought about *my* two queen sized beds at the Airport Coaster Inn.

There were no surprises in Mrs. Channey's bedroom. A double-sized bed stood in the middle of the room, a dresser on one side and a chest of drawers on the other. I like the newer trend of a chest and two nightstands. Those big dressers take up too much good vacuuming room.

"This is where Grandma sleeps. Since she's going to let you stay, it's where you'll sleep." He put my suitcase in front of her closed closet door. He sat on the made bed and looked at me like I was supposed to thank him or something.

"You sound like you got a problem with that?" I wasn't afraid of him, maybe I've got more nerve than it takes to live, but my instincts were telling me he was selling wolf tickets.

He smiled. "Yeah, you talk like one of Aunt Jan's friends. No, I ain't got no problems with you staying. But I do think it's odd that you would turn up now."

"Why?"

"I've heard about you, but in almost thirty years I haven't met you. Then you turn up when Aunt Jan is on the run. Just seems odd to me."

"So you're saying there's a better time to see a friend than when she needs me?"

He paused like he needed to think about what I asked. Finally he smiled in spite of himself.

"What can you tell me about what's going on, Glenn?"

He patted on the bed. "Come sit down. I wouldn't hit on a woman as old as my Aunt Jan."

I crossed the room and sat. Of all the reasons he could have used to say he didn't find me attractive, I figured "too old" was one of the nicer ones.

"For the record, Glenn, I'm three months younger than your aunt!"

"Excuse me, Miss Ruby." He smiled, a rather nice smile.

I looked him in the eye. Miz Audrey gave me one of those how-to-get-what-you-want books and I knew I needed to portray a right-to-know attitude. "Who do you think is trying to kill Jan?"

He laughed. "Where you from, baby, coming at me like Joe Friday?"

Baby? What is it about a bed under a man's ass that makes him talk mess? I reexamine Glenn. He was about six feet, solid, stocky built. His skin was dark with a touch of a reddish undertone. His features were pleasant, not as handsome as the picture Jan had of her brother, but I wouldn't have kicked him out of my bed. I mean if we were closer to the same age and I was back in my reckless days.

"I'm Ruby Gordon, from Petite, Tennessee. My friend is in danger and I want to know why? I'm willing to talk to you, Mr. Medicine Man and the devil himself if that's what it takes!"

His expression wasn't readable, at least not by me and my limited self. Maybe Dr. Gray would have had some fancy words to go with his eyes bucking like that and his mouth all dropped open. All I know to say is he looked like he didn't know if he was going to shit or go blind.

"Are you talking about Medicine Man, the Shiv?"

I smiled. "Have you got an Indian tribe living here in West Oakland?" I was going for the yuck, but his face was serious—dead serious.

"Don't be messing around with the Shivs. This family got enough troubles without some country girl stirring it up with them! I mean it! You don't know *a thing* about an Oakland gang."

I expected his loudness to bring Mrs. Channey. But the music I was hearing from the soap opera made me think some serious passion was probably playing out on the screen.

"Maybe you think you know too much." I said.

"What?"

"You people are so afraid of these kids, you probably forget that they *are* kids."

"Those little assholes have never been kids. They're underage, but don't ever make the mistake of thinking that means a young heart beats in their chests. There is no heart, there's no soul, no conscience—got it?"

Before I could answer the screaming poet, I really liked his way of speaking, Mrs. Channey's voice filtered in over the hum of the television.

"Glenn, you kids play nice in there," she hollered. I don't know if she was trying to be funny or if that's how she saw us, but it calmed Glenn down. He smiled again.

"I'm sorry, Ruby, I'm not usually the shouting types. I just don't want to see you or anybody else get hurt." He stood.

"I understand, don't worry none about me." I thought about Emerald and crossed my fingers before I added, "my mother didn't raise no fools."

"That's probably means a lot in Tennessee, but you don't have to be a fool to get killed in Oakland, you just need to be in the wrong place at the wrong time. I've got to get back to work. I come home on my lunch hour to check on my grandmother. You'll be here later?"

"I'm going back out, but I expect to sleep right here." I patted the bed I was still sitting on.

53

SEVEN
♠

Mrs. Channey seemed tired when she came up out of her soap opera haze. She talked a little about Glenn, called him a good boy (he's thirty-one); she talked a little about her other daughter, Pam, called her a victim of love (sounds a fool to me); and she talked a little about her son-in-law, Dante (called him an asshole). It was work getting her to tell me where to find Medicine Man, but I wore her down and she gave me directions. The house he rented was two blocks over; she said I couldn't miss it. She called it the biggest eye sore on the street. I couldn't wait to see a home she could afford to judge so harshly. She gave me Jan's number and told me to let it ring once, hang up and then ring it again. I promised her I would call her back, especially if I decided to stay across the bay with Jan.

I noticed when I stepped outside that kids were starting to show up. They were the youngest of the students, maybe half-dayers. A woman, every bit as old as Mrs. Channey, was next door working in her yard. She didn't seem to have a problem with staring at me in the same rude way Glenn had. I guess you can call it habit, but I went around Mrs. Channey's yard and picked up a few candy wrappers and other stray pieces of paper before I started my journey. I'm clean, what can I say? And it's hard to ignore somebody working as

54

hard as the old woman next door was working without doing your small part.

"You that girl I saw coming in with a suitcase?" She asked, as I passed her house.

"Yes Ma'am."

"You must not be one of those Channeys."

"Why do you say that?"

"You weren't blind to that trash like Nadine Channey's kin are. Where you walking to?"

I knew I wasn't in the south, but there's only so much rudeness I'm going to take, even from an old woman. You just don't be standing around having conversations with people without first introducing yourself, it's a mama's job to teach that.

I extended my hand. "I'm Ruby Gordon, from Petite, Tennessee, Ma'am." She ignored my hand, the old ass bitch.

"I'm Thaddie Stovall, folks call me Mother Stovall."

For some reason that made me want to laugh. She said it like she might have been telling Barbara Walters during an in-dept interview, "I'm Debbie Fields, folks call me Mrs. Fields, I'm a cookie baking fool." But I've been told I don't know when to laugh. I held it in.

Mrs.—Mother Stovall had been a big strapping woman in her day. I had watched her out of the corner of my eye as I'd picked up the yard. I'd say her body moved uncomfortably with its new thinness. She thrust herself with too much force when she moved and each time it knocked her off balance. I had a great-aunt who got old, forgot to eat and dropped about fifty pounds. She had the same problem. Mother Stovall was about five-five. I'd bet her longish thick white hair had been dyed red at some early point in her life. If she had been young today, it would've been blond. There was longtime attitude in the way she looked at me.

"You never did answer me about where you're walking to."

"It's a nice day for a walk, wouldn't you say?"

"This is California, it's always going to be a good day for a walk, but it's not a nice neighborhood for a walk. This ain't the killing zone, but we have our problems over here to." There was more edge to her voice than my mother has when she's talking to me about being a maid. I'd be damn if I gave her any more than she was willing to give me.

"Thank you. I'll be careful." I smiled my sweetest smile.

"No, you're not one of those Channeys, got too much sense. Well take your walking self on." She turned her back to me, dismissing me. I saw her bend down and swipe at an invisible weed.

"And you have a good day too." I swear, I've had enough of cranky old women to last me a lifetime. I wanted to hold up a big 'GET A MAN' sign to all of them. Pay him if you have to or, I wanted to tell them, take matters into your own hands. I don't care which just stopping taking it out on everybody else!

I've walked and worked in some of the best neighborhoods in Petite. I've even helped out at big parties in neighboring towns. I suppose somebody driving down this street would see me and figure I was walking home from the bus stop or the store, they wouldn't think anything of it. But I was terrified. What the majority people never seems to get is the only ghetto anybody ever feels comfortable in is their own. Take an Oakland brother who's down, put him in Harlem and he's scared, even if he never shows it. My cousin, who lives in Memphis, is a process server for a big insurance company. She grew up in Petite with me, but the people in her office can't seem to remember that. Whenever they have a subpoena that needs to be served in rough parts of the city, they think she's the likely one to take it out.

They say, "Garnet, I'm a little uncomfortable about this one will you serve it?" She used to do it, until her probation period was over. Now she'll look at the address and hand it back. "I don't feel good about this neighborhood either." Her supervisor tried to get an attitude about it, almost told my cousin that was the only reason they hired her, but they're in a union. Last I heard, with the exception of marginal evaluations, they haven't figured out a way to try to force her to do all the bad runs, but it's just a matter of time.

That's what I like about being self employed. When I reach the point that I know I can't wash another plate with the pattern of dancing ducks, I give notice; a week later, I'm somewhere else.

It's so different walking in a real neighborhood. The area I live in is less than twenty years old. Most of my neighbors are working class whites and working to middle class blacks, good people all. Their little lawns are neat and some of the big corner lots have roses and bushes and fancy walkways. As long as the people in my neighborhood stay working (which they probably will) and not become too prosperous to live there, it should stay nice for a while. But that won't happen. I already see "for sale" signs here and there. The market's not good right now. Some of those people who are trying to sell, so they can buy one of the new developments, will probably end up renting out. And it'll be the beginning of the end. I'm sure it's already started. It's probably what happened to Mrs. Channey's neighborhood. The sidewalks got me thinking about this. They weren't even and solid like the ones I'm now used to. They reminded me of the uneven sidewalks in the neighborhood where I grew up. There were big chunks missing in some, weeds growing up through them and cracks, big and small, on nearly every one—neglect. I'd forgotten what it's like to walk on sidewalks like this. Most of the places I've worked are so nice they don't even have sidewalks, which makes no sense at all.

The homes on Medicine Man's street were small like Mrs. Channey's. The street was quiet, not a little half-dayer in sight. I don't know if I was spooking myself or what, but it seemed unnaturally quiet. Like there were people standing just inside the doors, maybe peeking out the big picture windows, waiting for something to happen. I was reminded of a movie I saw about Vietnam. Some soldiers and some Vietnamese people were walking down a road. All of a sudden the native people started separating themselves from the soldiers, moving back into the rice fields, disappearing. A few moments later the American soldiers were attacked by the Cong. How did the natives know? And why didn't the American soldiers see what was happening? Was I walking into an ambush? No, that wouldn't be the right word. If I was walking into anything it was of my own making; hadn't anybody sent for me.

Mrs. Channey described Medicine Man's house as being in the middle of the block. She was right, it would've been hard to miss. The house was a dirty pale green that somebody had started repainting a darker green. Apparently they ran out of paint a third of the way into the job and had forgotten where they bought the paint. The job had to have started and ended at least a year ago. The new paint was weather-worn, the old paint was peeling and cracked. The yard was about fifteen small patches of weeds in a dirt field. There was an old Eldorado rusting out in the driveway. It was on blocks, which meant the garage door was blocked and inoperable too. I thought out a plan, but as I stepped up on the steps, I had my doubts.

A little fellow snatched the door open before I had a chance to knock. He looked all of ten, except for the goatee. I noticed he kept half of himself hidden behind the door.

"You a Witness?" he asked, before I even had a chance to say hello. He craned his neck around and looked to both sides of me. "Naw, you ain't no Witness. You by yourself. They annoy people in twos. Whatever you're selling, we ain't buying." He tried to close the door and I blocked it with my foot.

"I'm here to see Medicine Man," I shouted, as I removed my foot before he could open the door and slam it, like I would if someone blocked my door.

He closed the door. I could hear mumbling on the other side. It opened again.

"Who's calling?"

"A friend of Jan Channey's."

He closed the door again.

"I can take a message." This time it was a bigger guy with as much of a baby face as the first one.

"No, I need to talk to Medicine Man." The bigger guy closed the door. I heard some familiar noise. When I was a kid and my mother heard these sounds coming from my brother's room she'd hollered, "stop that roughhousing up there!"

The door opened all the way. The little guy was back and he was out of breath. I figured he and the bigger guy had done a quick-pick-up, but if that was true I'm glad I didn't see the room before they opened the door. "Come on in, it's going to take a few," he said.

There were three guys sitting at a card table in what was probably the dining area. But I couldn't focus on the humans too long. Medicine Man's house was filthy. There were overflowing ash trays, windows dirty with a kind of black smut, hand prints on the walls near the light switches. The brown carpet looked like it was speckled there were so many tiny pieces of paper in it. I had to move a crumpled newspaper to sit on the sofa which, surprisingly, looked new under the trash.

I would have preferred a hard back chair, which is where a person should sit when they suspect roaches, but the only hardbacked chairs were at the dining room table. The boys . . . men, sitting there didn't look like they'd appreciate my company. I couldn't tell what they were doing. There was a pad of paper with a drawing on it and a lot of lines. If I didn't know I was sitting up in the gang man's house, I would have figured them to be students, working out a geometry problem. I wasn't ten feet from the table and I knew they were talking, but I couldn't make out many words. One of them kept saying, "you understand?" and the other two would answer by nodding or mumbling, "got it."

I tried to read one of the crumpled papers, just to put my mind on something else, but the dirt around me was giving me the willies. I waited almost twenty minutes not that I wear a watch, but I'm good at estimating time.

Finally one of the men at the table went to the back, when he came out he said, "follow me."

I stood to follow, but he didn't move. He looked at me like I had been sitting on his puppy. I was tempted to look back down at the sofa.

"You strapped?" he asked.

I looked down at myself. Strapped? I had to think that one out. My first thought was that he was telling me my bra strap was showing. That wasn't the case. No, even after thinking longer, it didn't make sense. "I don't know what you mean," I told him.

That annoyed him, like I was stupid and wasting his time. Like he had to get back to the geometry lesson.

"Have you got a gun on you?"

I laughed. "No, child, I don't have a gun!" Why did I say that? I think he would have rather I pulled a big ass gun on him than call him "child." And I wouldn't have said it if I had thought it out, because all the "junior bird-men" (a name my mother uses for skinny men in short pants) had been strutting around, in their big baggy pants falling just below their knees, like they'd been hearing good things about themselves.

"My name is Oz. That's the only name I answer to!"

"All right, Oz. I'm Ruby Gordon, from Petite, Tennessee." He looked at me like he didn't care if I was Medusa from West Hell. He started walking and I followed. I wondered how he knew it was time to ask me to come back.

He knocked on the left side of a double door. A nice set of doors, oak wood I believe, I couldn't tell. They needed a good wiping of Murphy's oil, even plain water and some spray wax would have been an improvement.

I must say Medicine Man's office was a surprise. The windows were almost as dirty as the living room's, but everything else was neat. There was a big desk with a computer on it and a few pieces of paper. There was a two-shelf bookcase in one corner and there were about fifteen books in it. There were frame posters from the movies Menace to Society and The Five Heartbeats, one of which didn't make sense to me. Medicine Man was nowhere to be seen.

I heard a toilet flush and then some tap water running (a good sign) and a door opened. He was rubbing a sweet smelling lotion on his hands. He was wearing long pants and he looked like Eddie Murphy. He didn't look enough like Eddie to earn a little extra change as a celebrity impostor, but enough to jump-start my old heart. What a lot of folks don't know about me is I love me some Eddie Murphy. I'll go see one of his movies by myself. This Medicine Man walked across the room with the same sense of importance as my Eddie, like he was saying, "Yeah, it's me."

"You've got two minutes, start talking."

That wasn't the nicest greeting in the world, but I knew I meeting a hoodlum—Eddie Murphy-style or not. Folks that walk into a snake den and don't expect to find snakes are fools.

"My name is Ruby Gordon, from Petite, Tennessee. I have two questions. Are you after my friend Jan and if you're not who is?"

"Sit, Miss Gordon." He waited until I'd done so before he did.

"I've already talked to Rasan's mother about this matter. What's your interest?"

"She's my best friend. She's in trouble and I'm here to help."

"How?"

I leaned in and looked him in the eyes like Miz Audrey is always saying I should. "I'll help her anyway I can."

He pushed his chair back a little and let his right-hand drop from the desk. "I hope, for your sake, you're not saying you came into my house strapped?"

I smiled, proud because I knew what he meant. "No, Mr. er, what do they call you?"

"Man, just call me Man."

"No, Mr. Man, I'm not armed. I just came here for answers."

"You came from Tennessee?"

"That's right."

"Didn't have any other reason?"

I shook my head.

"That's deep. And the two of you are just friends?"

"We met in college."

"College, uh? Look, I like Rasan and I like his mother. I'm not involved in anything that would threaten or interest either one of them."

"Then who is?" I asked. I noticed he still hadn't brought his right hand up.

"I'm not one of Dionne Warwick's friends, but I'd guess it's somebody who wants them to believe it's me. I'm going to tell you like I told her, if you find out, let me know, but you come back personally and tell me. You tell Jan she must never again send anybody to my door in her name."

"I haven't seen Jan yet, she didn't send me."

"Do you know who I am?"

I nodded.

"And you came anyway?"

I nodded again.

He brought his hand up. "That's really deep, Miss Gordon. I could use some friends like you." He stood, dismissing me, these

Oakland folks weren't going to go down in my book as the friendliest.

"Mr. Man?"

"Just Man is fine."

"Okay, Man. I'll do something nice for you if you do something for me."

He smiled. He looked at me up and down and then threw his head back laughing.

I didn't appreciate that. I think I knew what he was thinking and it wasn't that damn funny.

"What will you do for me and what are you asking of me?"

"I'm a maid."

"A maid?"

"Right, a maid."

"And you're proud of that?"

"I'm self-employed and dealing in a service. It was my understanding that that's who you are too." There was a layer of this man/child, just under the surface, who wanted to relax and be a child—I could just feel it.

He smiled that Eddie Murphy smile again. "Touche'. Okay, you're a maid. What does that mean to me?"

"I'd like to give you an hour or two of my expertise. And for those two hours you'll continue to watch out for Rasan and his family."

"I can't make any promises like that. I'm not in the protection business."

"But you'll give me your word that you'll do the best you can?"

"That's all you want? Suppose it means I have to hurt somebody?"

"When I go in there to clean your house, I won't need any cleaning tips from you."

He grinned. I think he liked my answer. He pushed a button on a machine next to his computer. There was a knock at the door. Oz came in when Medicine Man said, "enter." It reminded me of that bald-headed Star Trek actor that Emerald loves so much and, again,

I had to fight off the giggles.

"Miss Gordon is going to clean up a little around here. You and the rest of the guys are taking orders from her for the next two hours. Send Manuel to the store for anything she needs." Oz looked like he wanted to protest, but thought better of it.

"One more question?" I asked before leaving.

"What?"

"Why do they call you Medicine Man?" I asked.

"That's an easy one. When I was a kid, I used to have what you might call an independent neighborhood pharmacy."

When was that, last year? I asked myself. I wondered how many days, months, years this child had left before the next bigger/badder Medicine Man would kill him and take his place. He was a person who could have been the CEO of large company in another time, place, and maybe another skin.

The next ninety minutes were some of the hardest and most satisfying in my career. I enjoy cleaning things that actually show a difference. I started with the windows. Naturally the junior bird men didn't have any window cleaner, but they had a coffee can of condiments from various fast food restaurants. I used six packets of vinegar, from a fish place, mixed with three cups of water in a big plastic mixing bowl to wash the windows. I got chills when the clean windows emerged from the smutty glass.

"How'd they get so dirty?" I asked Oz, who apparently had appointed himself supervisor of the two guys who were helping me.

He looked around, I guess to see if Medicine Man was in earshot. "There used to be a brother here who would hit the pipe when Man wasn't around."

"I've cleaned windows in a smoker's house before, this ain't regular smoke, unless he was in here smoking meat."

All the guys laughed. "He was smoking crack, sister."

"Just imagine what his lungs must look like?"

"That's not anything old boy has to worry about anymore," Oz answered. They acted like that was the funniest thing anybody ever said.

It made me want to cry.

Manuel returned with a bag of cleaning fluids and somebody's vacuum cleaner. After the windows and the kitchen, the rest was a breeze to do.

"How long do you think the house will stay this clean?" I asked Oz as I was leaving.

He frowned.

"Once Man sees it, I'd say forever. Thanks for nothing, Miss Ruby Gordon."

I laughed a little housework wasn't going to hurt none of them.

EIGHT
♠

I stopped at the liquor store to call Jan before returning to her mother's house. The telephone wasn't actually in the store, it was on the side of the building. A side that, apparently, served as the local restroom too. It's not easy to hold your breath and dial (actually push) a number at the same time. I was hoping I wouldn't have any trouble getting through. I'd already pictured, or as Miz Audrey says "visualized," myself telling the operator she had to dial the number, let it ring once, hang up and dial again. It went through the first time and I got nervous about getting it hung up before the second ring. Then I had to wait for my money to fall before I dialed it again. That's when I heard a mechanical voice say, "please deposit fifty-five cents." That confused me. Did the first ring count? Or was it a hang up at the mechanical voice center? While the telephone was ringing, I thought it out. This hang up stuff wasn't going to work from a pay phone. I let it ring about seven times before I decided to go back to Mrs. Channey's and reverse the charges to my home phone. I figured I would call Jan and tell her to call me back at the pay phone in ten minutes. I'd lost count of the rings when I heard her, "Port Dell Cafe."

"How did you know it was me?"

"Me who? Ruby?"

"Yeah, Girl, this is Ruby, standing in pee, outside your neighborhood liquor store, in Oakland, California."

She screamed and started laughing. "I know the spot well and probably know whose pee you're standing in. What are you doing here?"

"What am I doing here? You write me a letter like that and expect me to stay home? Your mother didn't tell you?"

"I called her this morning and she said you were on your way over, but I figured that was the rum talking already and what she meant to say was you called."

"I'm here and I'm coming over to see you. Tell me where you are."

Jan told me she was in Foster City, which I said sounded like a little town in Mississippi and she agreed.

"But wait until you see it, it sure doesn't look like one."

She told me how to take BART across the bay and then take a bus down the peninsula, but I had another idea. When we hung up, I called Jose's beeper number and left a message for him to call me at Mrs. Channey's.

♠♠♠

When I got back to Mrs. Channey's, I could see through the screen that she was asleep in her chair. The television was as loud as it had been, which I found almost impossible to believe she could sleep through. I put my hand through one of the big holes and undid the latch. I re-latched it. She didn't wake. I decided she wouldn't mind if I made myself another glass of cola. I went into the kitchen. I thought I heard voices at one point, but decided it was the television. When I turned to put the slushy cola back in the freezer, I felt something poke in my back. I screamed.

"Just step away from the refrigerator," it was a man's voice

I took one step back, still not turning, the pressure still in the middle of my back.

"Let me explain," I said.

"Shut-up and turn around slow-like."

Slow-like, I thought, what's like slow—kinda fast? I turned

around.

"Who is she, Dante?" It was a woman's voice from the dining room.

"I don't know yet, get back!"

When I heard the woman in the other room say Dante, I knew who was holding his finger in my back. I saw him when I turned. I like the name Dante it sounds young, sexy, maybe a little dangerous. I turned around and faced a big yellow mountain with freckles, sausage lips and a real gun in his hand. I couldn't believe it. I looked at the gun and turned to get a side view of it. I grew up around guns, my daddy worked security jobs, that was the smallest barrel I'd ever seen.

"What are you looking at? You think I won't use it?" he asked.

"What kind of gun is that?" I asked. I swear, what I'm about to say actually happened. The fool turned the revolver around and looked down the barrel. It was at arms length, but still? I almost laughed, but he quickly turned it back on me.

"What kind of gun is this, Pam?" he hollered.

"An NAA .22 short, why?"

He looked at me like he wanted me to answer, but I was starting to get an attitude about him pointing it at me.

"What are you doing in my mother-in-law's kitchen?"

"Dante, you better take that empty gun outta my face if you think you want me to answer your questions."

"Don't be calling my name, I . . . how do you know it's empty?"

"I'm looking at the barrel. Call Pam in here, she'll know me."

"Pam, she says she knows you!"

"I didn't say that, I-said-she'll-know-me!"

Pam peeked around the corner, so fast I didn't really see her. "I don't know her," she said from the dining room.

"I'm Ruby Gordon, from Petite, Tennessee. I went to college with Jan." I said it loud enough to wake up Mrs. Channey, or so I thought.

"College? Ump." He smiled like college was the lie-detector

word. He fixed a cocky look on his face. Pam entered the room. She was a slightly taller, slightly bigger, version of Jan. Way too cute for this Dante fool.

"Ruby?"

I nodded.

She opened her arms in front of the gun, still pointed at me, and leaned in hugging me. "Girl, I've been hearing about you forever." She turned to her husband, "Baby, put down the gun. This is Ruby, Jan's friend."

"What college did Jan go to?" he asked, pouting out the words. Or maybe with lips like those, everything looks like a pout. "How we know this is really her, have you seen pictures?"

I was just getting ready to tell him some things, about Jan, that only a very close friend or relative would know when the telephone rang.

"That's probably for me," I said, pushing his little gun out of my way and hurrying to the living room. I thought his grammar was bad enough to be in my family. And how does this fool figure Jan got to be an accountant without going to college?

"Hello, my name is Jose. I had a page to call this number."

"Jose, this is Ruby Gordon. Were you serious about helping me?"

"Sure, Tennessee."

"Good. I want you to take me somewhere, but I'll tell you where when you get here."

"Somewhere here in Oakland?"

"No, bigger than your favorite place."

He laughed. "Okay, then I'll assume you mean across the bay, because I'm not taking you across the ocean, no matter how much you look like Monique."

NINE
♠

Jose promised he would come, but he had to look up something at the library first. He had a paper due Monday. I used the time to get to know Pam and Dante. Pam was the sweet innocent Jan described her to be. She's at least five years younger than us, but somehow, like Jan, time hadn't messed with her as much as I feel it has me. She looked all of twenty and she had to be closer to thirty-seven, thirty-eight. She had clear light brown skin and big pretty teeth like Jan's. I learned she's been married seven years and last year she and Dante's Oakland hills home was destroyed by fire. I'd heard about the fire she was talking about, not from Jan, it was big news in Tennessee too.

They had an expensive home, even by California standards. Pam said it was really odd that their house caught afire, because the biggest block of homes that burned, near them, was four miles away. She said they'd only been in it eighteen months. Apparently, Dante's father died and they talked his mother into selling her house and moving in with them. They used the sale of her property for the down payment. I wasn't asking Pam any of her personal business. It was as if she'd been waiting to meet me, so she could tell me. I wondered if folks talked to the girl, she seemed so starved for conversation.

Usually people like that make me uneasy, but she reminded me too much of Jan for me to be bothered. As soon as Dante left the room, she leaned over and touched me on the leg. We were sitting on Mrs., Channey's bed, apparently the informal family room in this house. "Dante and I are trying to have a baby," she confessed. I say confessed because that's how she said it. Did she want me to leave the bedroom? I didn't know what to say.

"We'd been waiting to buy a house to get started and now it looks like we might have waited too long."

"I'm sorry to hear that."

"And I'll be a good mother too,"

"I'm sure you will." I hoped the baby looks like her.

"Yeah, I really want a baby, Ruby. My doctor says there's nothing wrong with either of us. She thinks there's too much tension in this house. You know, with the shootings and all. And my mother doesn't get along with Dante—never did."

I nodded. Jan's sister or not, she talked too damn much. Emerald says I have a sucker's face, that's why people always sit down and begin telling me their business, "It'll probably be all over soon," I offered.

She smiled. "That's what I'm hoping. Jan always said you were smart as a whip, wasting yourself cleaning other people houses,"

Smart or not, and I'd argue not, I'm just a maid. These people were putting much to much faith in me. What do I know about solving crimes? "What can you tell me about what's going on?" I asked, since she had brought up the subject.

"I think it's the Shivs. They told Jan it wasn't them, but why trust the word of a criminal?"

"What's their motive?"

"I don't know. Maybe it's a slow time in drug and gun sales. Do they really need a motive? What was their motive the first time they started dogging Rasan? Excuse my language, but they're little shits. I can't wait to get out of this neighborhood again."

I nodded. I could see she wasn't the type to take the hood in stride. "Could it be somebody closer?'

She had a look on her face like she never considered the idea. "Are you saying somebody like friends or family?"

70

I nodded.

"Of course not. We get along with everybody. My mother has been in this neighborhood since I was three." She paused like she was remembering something that would make her words a lie. "The only person I can think of, who doesn't like us, is our next door neighbor, Mother Stovall, and she's harmless."

I didn't think it was the time to mention that I'd met Thaddie Stovall and harmless is not the word I'd use to describe her.

"What about relatives?"

"That's just inconceivable to me."

"It happens."

"Not in this family, Ruby. There are five very different adults living in this house right now, we get along pretty well."

"And those outside this house?"

"Same thing. We have cousins, aunts and uncles all over the East Bay. We're one big happy family."

"Okay, You're probably right. I have a friend picking me up in a little while. I'm going out front to talk to your mother."

"Tell Dante to come here, will you?"

"Sure."

Dante was sitting on the sofa with the remote in his hand.

Mrs. Channey was reading the TV listings magazine. I could feel the chill between them. With him holding the remote and her looking up something to watch, I figured the showdown was just seconds away. He smiled at me when I walked in. At first I thought it was an apology smile, but then I recognized the "old dog's leer." It's that look whorish men give any woman between twelve and the grave to let them know they're willing to entertain any thing she can come up with. Pam deserved better, especially since she seemed to think she had better

"Your wife wants you," I told him, not looking at him, pretending to notice something on the television.

"I'm not surprised. That woman can't stand to have me out of sight." He smiled, as he struggled to get up from the couch.

"That's because she knows she can't trust him as far as she can throw him," Mrs. Channey mumbled, as soon as he rounded the

71

corner. I laughed. I hadn't heard that expression in a long time. I told her I was waiting for a ride across the bay. She shushed me, and bobbed her head toward the back. I figured she was either saying meet me in the kitchen or I was going to have to see her yard again. I started walking in that direction and thought she was behind me. When I got to the kitchen, I could hear her coming. She entered the room with an umbrella in her hand.

"Let's go outside," she said. She didn't say anything until we were both planted on that bench again,

"You're going to see Jan?" she asked, looking around like we were in a spy movie, meeting on the Capitol Mall.

I nodded.

"Here, give this to my baby." She reached into her bra and brought out a bill. I unfolded it, It was a ten-dollar bill folded to postage stamp size. I smiled, it reminded me of something my mother would do. Why do old women fold up money like that and slip it to you like they're passing drugs?

"I don't know what she's doing for money," Mrs. Channey added. I didn't know either, but I figured if the best her mom could come up with was this wrinkled ten, she'd need to continue doing it.

"And I want to give you this," she handed me the umbrella, a red, black and green automatic, with a black handle.

"Is it supposed to rain?" I asked, searching for a cloud.

"I don't know. I don't pay no never-mind to the weather reports, but I take one of my umbrellas every time I go out."

"Okay, why?"

"See." She unfastened it and pushed the metal tab. I expected it to pop open, it did jump out long, but the fabric didn't fan out. I looked at Mrs. Channey, surely I was missing something.

"See, Ruby." She pointed to the tip of the umbrella. There was a piece of metal, about an inch long, sticking out of the top.

"Watch." She jabbed at a leaf that had worked its way from one of Mother Stovall's trees. She speared it, reminding me of one of those men in orange jumpsuits you see jabbing trash on the side of the freeways. She smiled like she had speared a whale. "I haven't had to use one yet, but you saw how fast it opens?"

I nodded.

"The way I figure it, all you have to do is point it at the little punk and push this small button. Bam! He's bending over in pain and you're making dust." She sat back down, smiled, and rocked like she'd just told me the secret of life and maybe she had.

I took the refolded umbrella from her. "You have more than one of these?" The thought maid in the shade was running through my mind and I was fighting the giggles.

"Yup, it's funny how you always end up with more umbrellas than you can remember buying."

Actually I had the opposite umbrella problem.

"After this one broke and I saw what it was. I made two more. I take them everywhere. I'd like to see somebody try to tell me I can't carry an umbrella. Pam told me I couldn't carry that pepper spray Jan bought me, but how are they going to stop me from carrying an umbrella? Telling me I had to take a class to spray some little asshole with my pepper spray . . . "

She was working up to a stew. I decided to change the subject. "Mrs. Channey, how do Jan and Dante get along?"

"Girl, don't get me started on him. How's Jan going to get along with him? You and I both know she does not suffer a fool."

Knowing Jan, and having met him, it *was* a dumb question. The Jan Channey I knew had no patience for stupidity. "What's the story on Mother Stovall?"

"You've met her?"

I nodded.

"Figures, she can't stay outta our business. Did she ask you a lot of questions?"

"A few."

"I don't have anything to say about Thaddie Stovall."

"Do you think she could somehow be involved?"

"I wouldn't put anything past her." She locked her jaws and I knew I wasn't going to hear anything else about Mother Stovall in that conversation.

"I better get out front. My friend should be here soon."

"I didn't know you knew anybody else out here."

"I met him yesterday."

"What?"

"He's just a really nice kid who wants to help."

"Child, those words don't even fit together in this city." She saw the confusion on my face and explained. "I mean the words nice, kid, and help."

I'm glad I'm from a small town. I hope my environment never gets so bad that I have to suspect everybody. "I'll be careful."

"Before you leave, I'll have Pam take down his license number. If I don't hear from you by this time tomorrow, I'll call it in to the police. Not that they'll do a damn thing. That black newswoman, on channel three, her mother goes to my church. I'll call her if I need to get some real attention."

"All right, but I'm sure he's all right."

We went back into the house. I thought I heard shouting coming from the back, but Mrs. Channey didn't seem to notice.

I saw the blue CRX, through the picture window, as soon as I entered the living room. Jose was getting out of the car. I thought about going to meet him, but decided it might help ease Mrs. Channey's mind to meet him. I couldn't blame her for being suspicious.

"He's here," I hollered to Mrs. Channey, who was still in the kitchen.

"Pam!" Mrs. Channey called out.

I gathered up my purse and clutched the umbrella under my arm.

"You better take a jacket," Mrs., Channey said.

I was thinking that too, but I didn't want to disturb Pam and her husband. They could have been back there working on that baby. Pam came out with Dante a few beats behind her. Jose was just getting to the screen. Pam saw him and jumped back behind the doorway. Dante peered over her and went to the door.

"I'll be right with you, Jose," I said, dashing to the bedroom. "He's okay," I said to Pam, as I passed her.

I heard Jose say, "How'ya doing?" to Dante, but I didn't hear Dante's response.

I took my neon green windbreaker jacket from my suitcase. I took two fifty-dollar bills out of my running shoe. I was tempted to take all of it, had planned to take all of it, but Mrs. Channey had raised slight doubts in my mind about Jose. But Dante struck me as the type to go through a suitcase. I got my keys out and locked the suitcase. I didn't want to offend anybody, but they'd have to try to open it to know I locked it. The only person that could be offended would be, at best, a snoop. I put the umbrella in my purse.

Jose was still standing on the porch when I came out.

"I'm ready," I told him, trying to ignore the question in his expression. No doubt Dante or maybe Mrs. Channey said or did something strange, but I could wait until the car to hear about it. I noticed Mother Shovall was staring out her screen as we drove away.

"I'd expect your friends to be friendlier," he said, as we turned onto West Grand Avenue. Everything looked different, not as clean, as it had when we passed the first time, but I was sure he was going the same way.

"Were they rude?"

"Not exactly rude, just not . . . friendly—I can't think of anything else to call it. The old lady kept asking me about my people. At first I thought she was trying to figure out if she knows them, you know how old people will do that?"

I nodded, did I ever. My mother figured if she didn't know something about a black person she was meeting, then that person was lying about being from Petite. And there must be a few thousand African Americans in town.

"But then it seemed like she was just getting information so she could trace me if she had to, or maybe contact my next of kin." He laughed, but I didn't,

"It's not as strange as it seems. I believe they're probably nice people, but their home has been fired on a few times and, like I told you, Jan's life has been threatened."

"Yeah, not a good time to meet strangers."

At 13th and Broadway, we passed a group of people waiting for the 82, or the 8LL, or so read the bus stop sign. They looked just like bus stop people I would expect to see in Petite or anywhere else, except about half of them weren't black or white. They were Asian and brown and every imaginable combination of the four.

"What's that?" I asked.

"The federal building."

I smiled. Jan would love this tan and gray monstrosity (a word she used often to describe ugly buildings). It was just the kind of building she would get off a bus to study.

"Why does your car keep making those bird sounds?"

"That's not my car." He smiled, he was going to make me ask the next question.

"Okay, Jose, what's making those bird sounds?"

"Aren't they cool? See those little speakers on the crossing lights?"

I looked up as we passed one. He was right, there were speakers on the lights, "What are they?" I asked.

"Alarms for blind people, so they'll know when to cross." He sat back, smiling like he'd thought of it,

"I never would have expected to see so many signs in Chinese outside of China."

"Wait until we get to San Francisco. That reminds me, how do you feel about bridges?"

"They're okay."

"You have no fear of them?"

"I don't like them, but that's not a problem because I've been able to avoid them."

"Well, you're about to have your moment of truth. I can take the Bay Bridge, its right here and you'll get to see part of the city. Or I can take the San Mateo Bridge, which is right across the bay at Foster City."

"Which is easier?"

"The Bay for immediate convenience, the San Mateo for once-we-get-off convenience. If you fear bridges, the Bay bridge is your best bet."

"Why?"

He looked like he was straining to find the right words. "I'll tell you what, I'll take the San Mateo back and you'll see what I

76

mean."

"Okay." We turned onto the freeway and I noticed the sign "toll crossing."

TEN

♠

I swear to all that is holy, I've never been so frightened in all of my life and I've been mugged. I didn't know I didn't like bridges, maybe on some level I suspected it, because, like I told Jose, I've avoided bridges for the most part. Maybe on some inner soul level, I knew I had to stay the hell away from them.

After we entered the freeway I expected to see water. Jose explained to me that those signs were found at the opening to the bridges going both ways. I saw some booths that looked like those turnpike booths you find driving up north from the south. A young black woman stuck out her hand for the money, but didn't stop her loud conversation with the woman in the toll booth next to her.

I told Jose, forcing the ten-dollar bill Mrs. Channey had given me into his right hand, "It's on me. Put the rest in the tank." I figured I would give Jan one of the fifties.

"I pay my way, Ruby."

"I'm sure you do, but this ain't your way. It's my way and you're doing it for me. And let me know when you're ready to eat too."

"I can't even buy you dinner? You're a cheap date, Tennessee."

"Darling, if I'm any kind of date for you, you're spending way too much time working and studying."

He started laughing, I'd hoped he would. "I knew you were like Monique when I first met you.

"So are you ready to tell me about this foolish Monique woman?" I didn't care what he talked about. I saw that big steel gray bridge stretching out in front of me and I just wanted him to fill the car up with words to keep my fear from surrounding me.

"Why do you call her foolish?" he asked truly shocked by my words.

"You keep talking about her in the past tense. I don't care if the Noble Prize committee has got her lined-up for the big one, sister-girl is foolish." Don't let nobody tell you Ruby Gordon can't flirt. I learned at my mother's knee. My mother is a woman that doesn't know a Coke bottle from a baseball bat most of the time, but let a man enter the room and she's a genius with her flattery and eye-batting. When I was a kid, tagging along next to her in her bright shirt-waisted summer dresses, she'd flirt with the butcher, green grocer, cleaner's guy, black, white, Greek or freak—it didn't matter. My father was amazed by the amount of ground round my mother could buy with a dollar, the amount of clothes she could have cleaned with two, and so on. I doubt if she ever went beyond flirting, but sometimes I've wondered.

Jose got quiet and the thought ran across my mind that the girl was dead. It wouldn't have been the first time my big mouth got me in trouble.

We actually entered the bridge. There were seams in it that felt like they were going to give way every time we rode over one. They were about two or three car lengths apart.

"I don't like this, Jose," I finally said aloud. I was afraid the words would send me into a panic attack, something that I hadn't had in two years. A time in my life I don't like to think about.

"Uh, what?" He jerked like I had awakened him.

"Is it much longer?"

Before he could answer I saw a sign that said Treasure Island and I could see we were almost back on land. I touched his hand.

"I'm okay, I guess I do fear bridges. Is the San Mateo worst than this one?"

79

He reached down and held my hand, he squeezed it. "Ruby, it's not over."

"What's not over?"

Again, before he could respond the answer was revealed. This Treasure Island was in fact, an island. It looked liked we had more to cross then we'd already crossed. "Oh my God!"

"Will it help to close your eyes?"

"I don't think so?"

"What about looking at the skyline or the water?"

"No, definitely not the water." Up to that point I'd been avoiding that view. I looked down and felt Mrs. Channey's cola rise up. It burned in my throat and I swallowed hard to keep it down.

"That was really nice what you said," Jose began. "I guess I'm so far from where I want to be, I forget that I'm on my way."

Somehow, Jose had figured out that he needed to talk to me to keep my mind off of what was happening. "What do you mean?"

"Monique was older, five years. She used to fly up every couple of weeks from L.A. I'd meet her at the terminal, like I did you, and take her to the hotel. The first few months she would sit in the back and tip me five dollars when we got to the hotel."

Damn, did I tip him? I couldn't remember.

"I knew I was making progress when she started sitting in the front. My happiest day with her was the day she didn't tip me."

"Why?"

"I knew she was thinking of me like a friend. The next time she came up she asked me if there was anything to do near the hotel, she said she wasn't tired. It was my last run. I had about a half hour of paperwork to do and I was off. I asked her if she wanted to go out and was shocked when she accepted."

That's a man for you. Clearly she was asking him to take her out, how do they miss such obvious clues?

"We had a really good time, I ended up spending the night in her room. It's funny, after working there for three years, that was my first time sleeping in one of their rooms, but it wasn't the last time,"

The skyline was getting closer. I saw that pointy building you always see in pictures of San Francisco. I wondered what Jan

Channey thought of it, did it qualify as a good building by her standards?

"It won't be long now, " he said.

"I know." He was holding my hand again and, as ridiculous as it sounds, I didn't want him to stop. He might be young enough to be your child, I reminded myself. "How old are you?" I blurted out. I didn't mean to blurt, but we crossed over one of those seams just as the words were leaving my mouth.

"Guess. "

God, I was hoping he wouldn't say that. I hate to guess ages. I'm terrible at it, especially with black men, who never seem to age. "Well, let's see, my daddy is seventy-seven and I figure you're younger than him. Am I close?"

"Jeez, I'm thirty-one. Older than you thought, right?"

"Yeah, actually you are. I figured with you being a student and all, twenty-five tops."

"I blew off a few good years, but I'm on the right track now." He looked at me and smiled. I wanted to scream, "watch the road," but there was something kind of sweet about it. He made me wish I had a younger sister I could introduce him to and then I remembered I do have a younger sister. So much for that introduction,

"Monique was freaked by the bridges too."

"Maybe we were separated at birth."

He laughed a little too hard.

"Don't tell me, that sounded like something she would say?"

He nodded.

I can't say I saw much of San Francisco. We made a series of turns in what was probably downtown and the next thing I knew we were heading south on the 101 freeway. He pointed out Candlestick Park and I was surprised I knew that the 49ers played there. He talked about the Raiders (his team) and trashed the 49ers (called them a yuppie, buppie team) and he played his favorite tape for me. It was an old Johnny Gill tape and he was surprised I recognized it. We passed through about four or five cities and he called out the names of all of them.

It was so different from traveling in the south, where you

leave one little town and you don't see much until you get to the edge of the next little town. If he hadn't said anything, I could have believed the twenty or so miles we traveled after exiting the bridge was all San Francisco. As we approached the San Francisco airport, he said he wanted to show me the Peninsula Coaster Inn, but I was getting too excited about seeing Jan Channey again, I didn't think I could pretend to care about looking at a hotel. I didn't want to disappoint him, I told him the truth and he thought it was very Monique-like of me. His comparisons were starting to wear on me.

"How do you feel about land bridges?"

Since I wasn't sure what he meant by that, I told him I was okay with them. "Why do you ask?"

He bobbed his head forward. "This exit coming up will take us into Foster City. My cousin, who lives in San Mateo calls it the back way."

It was an exit that crossed the freeway by going way up in the air and making a big curve. I gritted my teeth. He took the exit and it was every bit as scary as I expected.

"I'll drop you off and hang with my cousins while you visit with your friends. You can just call me when you're ready to go back."

"Maybe you better call to make sure they're there."

"Somebody is always home at my aunt's house. If my cousins aren't around, one of them will be showing up soon."

"This is so sweet of you."

"I hate that word, sweet."

"Why?"

"Sweet is a little boy, not ready for prime time."

I laughed. "Okay, this is a manly act, Jose. Thank you."

ELEVEN
♠

Now don't get me wrong, there are some nice towns in Mississippi, but within seconds of entering the city limits, I could see what Jan Channey meant when she said Foster City might sound like a town in Mississippi, but it didn't look one. Everything looked new, not just new, but sterile—just short of lifeless. It was all the way California. There was a mall visible, from the so-called back road, that looked like one of the store's ceilings was covered in a white tent.

"There's a lot of little man-made lakes or lagoons around here, but the bridges are really short."

"What does that mean?"

"Three, four car lengths and we're off."

"Do you know where her street is?"

"I think so."

He turned onto a street named Hillsdale. We were going so slow I thought he was reading the street signs, but that didn't seem to be happening either. Maybe I was just anxious, but it seemed like his driving was inconsistent.

"Why so slow?" I finally asked.

"You know how certain police in certain places have a

reputation for messing with a brother?"

Did I ever? Poor Raymond got stopped every other time he came into Miz Audrey's subdivision to pick me up. "I know."

"Foster City has that kind of reputation. Normally, I wouldn't sweat it, but I can't take the bust."

"Why not?" I knew this question was dipping into his business, but the man had brought me across a bridge.

"My license expired two weeks ago and I haven't gotten around to standing in the DMV line. It such a hassle." He looked at me, no doubt trying to gauge my concern.

"Belated happy birthday."

He smiled. "You're a classy lady, Tennessee."

When he said that, I tried to remember if I'd told him I'm a maid. We pulled onto a street that was nice. As shaded and manicured as any I've seen, yet simple in a My Three Sons neighborhood kind of way. We started looking for the address.

"Your side," Jose said. We both started reading off the numbers on my side of the street. The house was on a corner lot. Not as pretty as some of the others on the street, but larger. He pulled into the driveway. Jan Channey appeared in front of us waving. At first I thought she was just waving, but she was trying to say something, Jose lowered the window. She came around to the driver's side

"Park it on the street, sweetie. My friend's company can't park in the driveway." She flashed her old Jan Channey smile at Jose and I knew my time as the classy old broad in his life was limited.

"Is that your friend," he asked me?

"That's Jan Channey."

"Where is this college you two went to, that's where I need to transfer?"

Jan was standing by my door when I opened it. She was jumping up and down like the teenager she appeared to be. She grabbed me and hugged me hard.

"Oh, Ruby, it's so wonderful to see you. Step back let me look at you." I tried to step back, but as soon as I separated myself from her, she grabbed me again. Tears were running down her cheek. "No, don't move, let me just hug you. I'll look at you later." She was trembling as we rocked together in front this big-ass house in Foster City, California. "Let's get in before the neighbors call in an NIN

84

report, that's a niggers in the neighborhood alert." She grabbed Jose's arm like she knew him and started dragging the two of us to the back of the house.

"Jan this is my friend, Jose."

She stopped walking. We were standing in front of the garage, which had to be as big, if not bigger, than my house. "Let me get this right," she started, and I knew I was getting ready to hear some vintage Jan Channey stuff. "This is your friend Jose?" I nodded, grinning. "Okay. And you got into town when?"

"Last night."

"Did you know Jose before you got here?" She answered before I could. "I-don't-think-so.'' She pulled me and Jose closer and whispered. "So now, kids, the question is, after being here my whole damn life, how come I don't have a friend Jose?"

Jose was lost to Jan. The more things change, the more they stayed the same. Just like in the past, I was happy to turn him over.

He laughed so loudly, a stern-face middle-aged woman stepped out of the house and onto the screened back porch.

"Jan, the neighbors," was all she said before giving me and Jose the fish-eye and returning to the house. Jan laughed.

"That Penny, what a hoot, got to love her." I don't know if Jose knew Jan was being sarcastic, but I did.

"Follow me," she said as she entered a side garage door.

"Wow, this place is great,"

"I agree," I said. "This is the damn garage?"

Jan Channey laughed. "I wish Penny was in here to hear you ask that. She would freak." She laughed even harder. "No, this is the mothers-in-law's apartment. Even though the maid lives here, don't call it the maid's quarters."

We stepped into the main room. It was one large, very well decorated room. The colors were the orange, yellow and green of the Kente clothe drapes that covered the patio door and window. I could see there was a pool on the other side. There was African art and sculpture everywhere. Not enough to look junky, I hate that knick-knack look.

I don't know when I've seen a more tasteful room, and I

know tasteful—all maids do.

"What you're looking at folks is Feng Shui at it's best," Jan explained.

"Cool, I've heard of that" Jose said.

"I haven't, it sounds like a Chinese bike company. What is it and what could it possible have to do with this African room?"

"Don't start me to lying, all I know is, the owners of the house had two little Asian guys come in and make sure all the energy in the main house and out here was right. The owners are really into it. They had to buy a house that faced south and make sure the property didn't form a triangle, Every picture, statue, color has been carefully chosen. Believe it or not the owners are in their sixties, semi-retired and into every kooky thing associated with California living."

That got my little mind spinning. Wow, I thought, folks be out in California paying "experts" good money to show them where to hang pictures. I could do that. Hell, if the price was right, I would hang the pictures and them light a candle and then dance nude around it. I wondered what that would be worth on the California market. I tried not to laugh. Jan never did have a lot of patience for my laughing fits.

The maid's quarters were a living room/dining room/ study with an upstairs bedroom loft, which was probably over the actual garage.

"Needless to say, don't move anything around, fucking up the energy. Come on over here and sit down and let me bring you up to date." Jan started walking toward the big overstuffed white sofa and I followed. Jose moved toward the front door again.

"Give me the number here, I'll call you back with my aunt's number." Jan gave him a slip of paper she had, apparently, anticipated somebody would need.

I walked Jose to the door. "Do you feel all right with it?" he asked.

I nodded. "I think I'll be okay."

"I like your friend."

"I gathered that."

"Don't be jealous, Tennessee. She doesn't look and talk like Monique. I'll call you in a couple of hours," he told me, then he added. "If I have your permission to leave. You know I'm at your service."

"Get outta here." I playfully pushed him out the door.

Jan Channey was grinning at me when I started back toward the sofa. "He's the cutest little thing. Where'd you find him?" She said it like she was talking about a puppy.

"You know those vans they use at the airport to transport passengers to the hotels?"

She nodded and I told her everything about meeting Jose.

"I've got dibbs on him when you leave." Her expression became serious. "If I'm still alive."

"Tell me what's happening, Jan."

She let her head drop to the back of the sofa. She rubbed her eyes. "I'm so tired of being afraid."

Her voice sadden and frightened me. Jan Channey is the boldest, most adventuresome person I know. Fear is not a word I could associate with her. This was a woman who talked me into hitchhiking to New York from Maine. What should have been a scary experience is remembered as the most exciting time in my life. That was the seventies, and I wouldn't expect a vanload of peace-loving, acid-tripping hippies to be on the road offering rides today, but it didn't have to work out that way then either. Jan made it work. She knew which rides to turn down, what to say to the people we rode with and how to live for two days in New York with sixty-three dollars between us. This sad, frightened, Jan Channey was a stranger to me.

"I talked to Medicine Man."

Jan sat up. "You what?"

"I went over there. I ended up cleaning his house for him."

She looked like she didn't know if she wanted to cry or laugh. "Start at the beginning."

"I wore your mother down and she told me where he lived. I walked around there and a little guy answered the door."

"And he just took you back to Man?"

"No, they went through a whole dance at the door, but I charmed them."

"Like hell."

"Hey, you're not the only woman in town who can charm a little boy." I smiled, trying to keep it light, but she still had that worried look on her face.

"Don't let those short pants fool you, those are not little boys. I doubt if they've ever been little boys."

"You sound like your nephew."

That made her smile, "You met my Baby?"

"You call him your baby? How come I don't remember hearing you talk about him?"

"I used to talk about him all the time. Don't you remember when we had to go to court to get him?" She could see I was still confused. "His mother was using cocaine long before most black folks knew anything about it, a good ten years before it became crack."

"Baby, you used to called him Baby!"

"Isn't that what I just said?"

It seemed silly to try to point out where the conversation broke down.

"Did he take you through some changes?"

"He tried."

"He's very protective of Mama. One day I saw him knock Dante up against the wall so hard it cracked. Dante had mouthed off at her."

"So you're saying he couldn't possibly be involved in this threat against you."

There was shock on her face. "Baby? No, he would never do anything to hurt me or Mama."

I wasn't convinced, but I didn't push. "What about Dante?"

She didn't have to think about it, "Girl, knowing his family, I wouldn't put anything past him, but there's no motivation. We're not best of friends or anything. In fact, last year, he hit Pam in front of me and I pulled a knife on him. Would've used it too if Pam hadn't put herself between us,"

"She's got it bad, huh?"

"Yeah, only thing I can figure is, with those lips, the boy must know how to spend some quality time eating . . . ," she threw her head back to emphasize the words, "at the Y. What else could it be?"

I nodded. It probably was something silly like that. I've thought out this abusive relationship stuff. If he's not rich, and I saw no evidence of Dante having much, then these women had to be whipped on a sexual level. "You haven't talked to her about it?"

"Girl, you can't talk to Pam about Dante. She won't hear it. She's not exactly a genius when it comes to everyday matters, but she a flaming idiot where he's concerned."

"One word—Emerald," I commiserated (Miz Audrey's word).

Jan nodded with me. "Baby sisters, got to love them. I missed you so much." She was crying again.

This was one more time than I've seen her cry in twenty years.

"My life was already fucked and now this."

I didn't know what to say. She was still small enough to wear those pencil-legged jeans that used to dot our dorm room floor. There were slight smile lines on her face, but they disappeared when she started crying again, Her hair was in dreads, still thick, still so black it was almost blue. She was living in the sunshine, and, like the song says, everybody loves the sunshine. She looked like she should be on a talk show talking about her latest book or movie. And with all of that she was a numbers genius. Until that moment I hadn't realized that part of what I called love for my best friend was envy.

"What it is, Jan? How can I help?"

"Ever since I've been trying to stay alive, I've been wondering why I should bother,"

"Because you've got people out here who need and love you, that's why. Was something happening before all this came up?"

"I stopped working for the county. Before I came over here, I was working temporary jobs. No benefits, but I figured I needed a change, you know, get out and meet some new people. It was fun for a while, but the first three places I worked offered me a permanent job. They were paying for an accounting clerk and getting an accountant. The last place had me doing taxes. But I'm supposed to be smart enough to do their damn work, but too stupid to know what kind of work I'm doing?"

"Chuck it, come home with me. Start working for yourself."

"What do you mean? Who the hell do you think I've been working for all these years—a better society?"

"You could really work for yourself. Print some cards."

"I've got cards." She said laughing. "Everybody out here has cards."

"I'm beginning to see that."

"What do you mean?"

"It's nothing. But I don't see why you can't just be an accountant or keep books for small businesses in your own place."

"An office?"

"A home office, in Tennessee. Think about it?"

She smiled and looked at me with her old light in her eyes.

"I will. Maybe that's what's wrong, I've been too long in one place."

"Now, all we have to figure out is who's trying to kill you."

"Oh is that all?" She picked up a black satin throw pillow and hit me with it. Just in time for the woman she called Penny to walk in and see her.

She was stiff, probably in her attitude too, but her body was a board. She wasn't wearing a black and white uniform, but it was just a technicality. Her mind had been uniformed for years. She wasn't unattractive, but being a maid myself, I've got a real problem with maids who put on more airs than their employees. I used to work for some white people who vacation on Binimi. There were American maids down there who put on more airs than the Queen of England. Maids that bragged about their travel like they'd been footing the bills. They had kids in the best schools and their own vacation property—time shares usually. And the worst yet, maids who bragged about their employees accomplishments. This stick-up-her-ass Penny would have fit in well there. I'm not saying they had anything to be ashamed of, certainly not, but if doctors and engineers don't go out of their way to show off, what does a maid have to show off about?

"Jan will you be visiting with your friend much longer? I was ready for my break."

Jan laughed, openly laughed at the woman, but being Jan Channey she could get away with it.

"Ruby Gordon meet Millicent Marchette, also known as Penny."

"You're the only one who calls me that ridiculous name."

"Pleased to meet you, Penny," I said. "You have an exquisite place." I knew she would appreciate the word exquisite. She nodded, not sure if I was messing with her by calling her by a name she'd just called ridiculous and topping it with a compliment—I was. Being with Jan always brings the child out of me.

"Ruby and I have been friends since college," Jan added, apparently knowing her friend would respond to the word college.

"College? How nice."

Jan jumped up, surprising me and startling her friend. I haven't been around her in a while and I'd forgotten how abrupt her movements are sometimes. We'd be sitting having lunch and she would jump up and run out of the room remembering a book she left in her last class. It takes some getting used to.

"Let's go for a walk, Ruby."

I stood.

"There's a cute little park a few blocks over with a duck pond. We'll feed the ducks." Jan started towards the kitchenette and the telephone rang. She and Penny exchanged looks and I was again reminded that my friend was living in fear.

"Hello," Penny answered, her voice very professional, phony. She looked at me with a look that made me stop to see if my feet were leaving a dirty spot on the carpet.

"Yes, she is, just a moment," Penny looked at Jan. "It's a call for your guest."

I would have said something, but Jan gave me a look. I hate rudeness. Like Raymond says, "we need something to separate us from the animals." And don't think I don't know how to get somebody told, because I do. I know all the words and I like the way

91

some of them roll off my lips, but its does bother me that, like somebody said, you have to curse some woman (his mother) to curse a man. But that's just me going off on a tangent (my ex-doctor's words).

"Ruby, it's me, Jose. Everything okay?"

"Everything is fine." Except Penny was rolling her eyes at me and Jan looked like she was about to have a laughing fit.

"I can hang around here as long as I want. Call me when you're ready to book. Here's the number, 342 . . . "

I need a pen, I mouthed to Jan while I pretended to write in the air. I repeated the numbers aloud. Penny saw Jan looking for a pen and continued to stand there watching us like she was watching a stage play. I repeated the number to Jose again.

"That's it, Tennessee. I'll talk to you later." He hung up, with me still penless.

"I've got some bread crumbs, let's walk to the park," Jan said. She turned to Penny. "We'll be back in about an hour?"

Penny nodded. "I'll need to start dinner around then, that's fine."

Jan grabbed a cloth purse from the bookshelf and asked me if I was ready. I picked up my purse, still uneasy about not having written down Jose's number, but thinking he would call me again if too much time passed.

Jan surprised me by starting to the left of the door, but every time she spoke of the park she pointed or nodded straight ahead toward the driveway.

"I didn't think it was in this direction," I told her,

"It's not, really, but the sidewalk to it is over here. And I want you to look at this house from this side, it's huge."

She was walking slow, comfortably, unlike a woman on the run. I looked back at the house, she was right. It was more house than I'd want to clean. "Is Penny going to let you show me the inside?"

"Fuck Penny. I'll give you a tour and if her employers walk in they don't care enough to know I'm not her. But she's really a nice person, Ruby, just been up under white folks too long."

"I know she must be, I have reason to believe you only

associate with quality folks." I could see the park in the distance. We were standing in front of a fire station. "How did you meet her?"

"I was working in Daly City. She hadn't moved here yet. We were both taking BART every morning around the same time. You know how that goes?"

I nodded.

"When she told me she was a maid I thought about you and we bonded." Jan laughed, Bonded was not her kind of word. "And anyway, how many people do you know that could lend me clothes?"

I laughed. She'd answered a question I'd had since I'd first saw her. She looked neat, her blouse was expensive and her slacks were stylish, but it wasn't her style. I envy her size, always had. Over the years, one size fits all had come to mean one size fits Jan Channey and now, apparently, Penny, the other maid.

We walked leisurely, like two Foster City matrons who didn't have to use housework to get their exercise. Our surroundings were clean, upscale. My next life, I promised myself, I'll live in a neighborhood like this.

"This park was named after that congressman or house rep, whatever he was, that was killed in Jonestown."

"Really," I said. "I always thought of those people as being from San Francisco." We were moving closer to the lake, where I could see about twenty well-fed ducks.

"The newspapers call this whole area San Francisco, they probably call Petite Memphis sometimes in reports,"

"Nothing ever happens in Petite for the national papers to call it anything. You'll see when you come back with me."

"Maybe I will. I think I'd like to be in a place where nothing ever happens."

Jan took a big handful of bread crumbs and threw them in the water. It seemed to take all her energy.

"Let's sit." She led me to the stone bench as she asked, "you really think it's one of my relatives?" We both paused, apparently there was a fire somewhere nearby. "Somebody won't be having steaks from the gas grill tonight," Jan said, grinning.

"I don't know what to think. I do know it's usually a relative, that's what the stats tell us."

"Well, we need to look outside. I've thought about it, there's just not any reason for any of my relatives to want me dead. It's not like they stand to inherit anything, unless somebody got his eye on my boombox."

We both tried to laugh.

"Then let's look outside."

"What about the Shivs?"

"Same with them. There's nothing I do that should concern any of them. They don't have two years to invest in recruiting a single member, so it's not about Rasan. What could it be?"

"Did he try to hit on you?"

"Who?"

"Medicine Man,"

"No, not really. He was charming, but he's too cool for that—hitting on somebody's mother. I don't think he would've turned anything down though." She shrugged. "The boy has money and looks, he has more than his share of sweet young things."

"Still."

"No, Man's not interested. But he's a real cutie isn't he?"

"Reminds me of Eddie Murphy,"

"You and your Eddie. Give me Denzel any day."

"Denzel is cool, but I've got a feeling if you put ole Denzel in a bag and shake him up, Bryant Gumble would fall out."

Jan leaned into me and pushed as she laughed. "So what? I'd take Bryant too."

"Quiet is it kept, I'd take Bryant too."

We both cracked up like it was 1971.

"Tell me about the man that's been following you."

"You know, I've seen his face. I didn't tell my mother, but I have a sense that I know him."

"From where, a job, the neighborhood, school?"

"I don't know. Maybe on a picture somewhere. I've racked my brain."

"Tell me what he looks like."

"Nondescript. He's a big-face, brown-skinned guy.

94

TWELVE
♠

There certainly weren't as many people in front of the house as, I suspect, would have been in front of Jan's mother's house or even my house in Tennessee. Two Foster City police officers were holding back about seventeen neighbors. There were five women and two elderly men standing near me. Judging by their dress and lack of real concern on their faces, I would say, two of the women were maids. These were the women I approached.

"What's going on over there?" I asked.

"Don't know," the younger of the two commented. She had an accent, but her English was fine.

"I heard somebody say they got Mr. and Mrs. Nesbaum's girl." This one had an accent too, English, not Spanish like the other one, but she was as dark as me.

"No!" I said, causing both of the women to do a double-take at me. They had been looking straight ahead as they spoke.

"Do you know her?" they asked, at the same time.

"I've seen her around, at the store and the post office. I work for Dr. Gray." I pointed, in the direction of the thickest part of the neighborhood. They nodded, like they thought they knew or had heard of a Dr. Gray.

" I heard Mrs. Wycoff tell the police there were about six of your people standing in the driveway earlier today."

My people? It took me a second to realize what she was saying.

"They're probably looking for somebody to talk to. They took a picture of the lot of us a few minutes ago," the brown English woman continued.

I looked for Jan. She was worming herself closer, having made herself invisible in that way small women can. I bid my pink collar sisters good day and left. I got close enough to Jan to reached out and grab her arm. "Come on, Jan, we can't help her," I whispered.

"Ruby, if Penny's dead, it's my fault. They were trying to get me!" Her little body was shaking. I had images of her breaking away from me and screaming out something silly, something that would have her, and me, sitting in one of those Foster City cruisers.

"Jan, there's a cop over there looking at us." I tugged her arm. "Don't look now!" The cop was looking around the crowd of police personnel and onlookers. No doubt looking for good old Mrs. Wycoff, so she could identify us as two of the "six" that had been in the driveway. I smiled and waved goodbye to my two pink collar sisters.

It confused them, but they were polite enough to return the wave. The gesture threw the cop a curve. He paused and thought it out. I saw him inching toward the two women. I wondered how long it would take to determine there was no Dr. Gray in the neighborhood or, if there was, I didn't work there.

I didn't know where I was leading Jan. Away was my immediate destination. We approached Hillsdale again and turned right. I could see a McDonald's about a block and a half away but then I notice a Carrows restaurant not half a block from us.

"Why are we going in here?" Jan protested. "I can't eat anything right now."

"We'll sit and figure out what we need to do." But I wasn't saying I couldn't eat. Eating is what I do when I'm nervous. I was glad I brought my purse, even after Jan told me I wouldn't need it on our walk.

Jan never was much of an eater. I tried shadowing her eating style one whole week when we were students. I liked a boy who told a boy who told a girl who told Jan I was too fat for his taste. Being one of eighteen black boys at Burns, I was willing to do whatever it would take to go out with him. Right there in my dorm room I had a perfect specimen of slimness. What could be easier? I thought I would die of starvation that week. I finally decided I could wait until the taste of boys grew into the already demonstrated mature male taste for more curves.

The sign said "seat yourself," and we took a booth toward the back. "We'll take coffee right now," I told the waitress who brought menus to us. I think it might have come out rude, because she did a double-take. "I mean before we order," I added smiling.

"Still worried about everybody else's feeling," Jan said. She picked up a napkin, unfolded it and buried her head in it; silently sobbing until the napkin was saturated. "This is fucked up, Ruby." She spoke her words while reaching across the table for my napkin.

"I know it is."

"Fucked up."

"Big time." I waited for her to blow her nose, even that was small and dainty like her. "Right now, off the top of your head, tell me who's doing this,"

She looked up, jerking her head like some power-tripping teacher was saying, "look at me while I'm talking!" I thought I saw a flash of anger in her eyes.

"I don't know. Some asshole!"

"Give him a name."

"I really don't know!" The room around us grew silent. "Why are you asking me this? Don't you believe me?"

"Of course I believe you, Jan Channey."

She tried to smile, but it came across looking like she'd caught a whiff of a bad smell. "I guess you wouldn't come across the country if you didn't, right?"

"Wrong. I would come across country if I thought you were trying to kill somebody . . . and I'd bring a shovel."

I was trying to help, but that little declaration of friendship started her crying again. The waitress returned with a pot of coffee and a whole stack of napkins, I knew then we couldn't sit long, apparently we were attracting too much attention.

"I can take your order now," the waitress said, in the gentle voice of a good nurse.

"Try to eat something, Jan. He'll still be a SOB even if you make yourself sick from not eating." I looked up at the middle-aged (around my age) waitress. "Tell her," I asked the waitress.

The waitress fell right into step saying, "That's right, sweetie, there's always another bus coming."

Jan looked at me with her old dead pan expression. It's the look she used to give me when I was trying too hard; too hard to be funny, or cute.

"That's right and while we're waiting for that bus, we'll each take a BLT," I ordered. The waitress scribbled something down and patted Jan on the shoulder. There was pep in her step as she walked away.

"That should buy us some time. She'll tell everybody at the other tables that you just broke up with your boyfriend."

"You're wasting yourself at Miz Audrey's you know?"

"Right, starting next week I'm going to search the want ads under accomplished liar."

We sat for a few seconds without speaking. "Miz Audrey says that we were all born with all the answers we'll ever need."

"Is that right?"

"That's what she says."

"Then why did she spend all those years in school learning medicine?"

I laughed, "That's a good question, I'll ask her next time she tells me to look into myself for an answer."

Jan smiled. "Will she fire you?"

"No, she's not like that. You'll like her."

"You're not telling me the two of you are friends?"

"No, not friends, but she respects me. And I can't say that about most of the women I've worked for. She says her grandmother used to do day work. She said, that's what they used to call it, day work,"

"You're rambling."

"I know, I'm nervous, next thing you know, I'll be eating too much."

"I know that's right. Starting with two BLTs. I don't eat swine anymore."

"Pull it out." I advised. Then I thought about it. "Since when?"

"I was going out with a Muslim for a minute."

I laughed. "Are you serious?"

She nodded.

"Get out of here. Suit-wearing, bean pie selling, newspaper-hawking, Muslim?"

"All of that."

"What happened?"

"I couldn't be me. He told me I talked too much. He told me I should learn to keep some of my opinions to myself."

I couldn't help it. I got tickled and laughed in earnest. I just couldn't see ole Jan Channey with anybody who was a practicing Muslim or overly religious of any kind. Jan Channey was a shameless hussy of the first degree on a good day. On a shameless day she was, what? I don't know.

"Did you have sex with him?"

"What kind of question is that? This happened last year not when I was fourteen!"

"You know what I mean! Aren't they celibate until marriage or some such?"

"He never told me that part. But, now that I think about it, it took us almost two months to get to it." She paused, like she just remembered something. "Why are we talking about this? Ruby, Penny might be dead."

"She's not."

"Miz Audrey taught you how to be a psychic too?"

"No, but I don't want to think about a dead maid too, okay?"

"Okay,"

We sat in the booth for about forty-five minutes. We wrote out, on a napkin, the names of everybody she dealt with in the past few months. We crossed out about half of the names. They were the "no way, no how people." The people left on the list after that were her family members, the Shivs and Mother Stovall.

I ate my sandwich while Jan picked at the bread on hers. "Let's start with Mother Stovall, what's her story?" I heard Jan Channey crunch and wondered if she meant to eat the piece of bacon I was certain she was chewing.

"Mother Stovall hates my mother, not me. I guess, since I'm thinking about it, that she is capable of murder or anything else, but why? What's her motive?"

"Why does she hate your mother?" I heard another crunch, then I watched as Jan Channey brazenly pried open the bread and took out a strip of bacon. She grinned at me while she took a big bite. "It's weird old folk's business."

"Tell me anyway."

She swallowed and said, "my father was having an affair with Thaddie Stovall in the late seventies early eighties. He got sick and started taking high blood pressure medication. The medicine made him impotent. Mother Stovall accused my mother of slipping something in Daddy's food so he couldn't get it up for her."

I wanted to ask her if she was serious, but why would she be kidding around at a time like this? "That's some of the craziest stuff I ever heard."

"Told you." She was pushing lettuce and tomato slices around, no doubt looking for some more bacon. She found a piece and attacked it. "So, like I said, she wouldn't be trying to kill me. And if my mother's her target, why wait six years after my father's death?"

"Or shoot Penny?"

"Right." She was eye-balling my plate, but it was too late for her to get any bacon or so much as a crumb from me.

"I just thought of something," I said. "Jose, how's he going to find me? Suppose he goes back to the house and the police get him?"

"Let's call him."

"I didn't write down the number, remember?"

102

"You give me so little credit. Have you forgotten who you're talking to? Jan Numbers R Me Channey." She rattled off Jose's aunt's number, then, showing off, she said it again backwards.

THIRTEEN
♠

Jose wasn't satisfied with our description of what had happened. He insisted on driving past Penny's employer's house. The actual street was blocked, but we drove past the side street, circled the block and drove past again from the other end. Most of the police cars were still there, but the onlookers were gone.

"Do we know that she's . . . how do you know that she's, dead?" Jose asked.

Jan was in the front seat with him, I was in the back. I figured he might need driving directions from her and I was anticipating the drive back across the bridge. Actually I was anticipating it with my face buried in the limited back seat.

"There was an ambulance there earlier?" he asked.

Jan nodded.

"That's a good sign,"

"Why?" we both asked.

"She must have been alive, then?"

I heard the question mark and answered. "You're right, I know they send ambulances for bodies too, but they don't rush away with them."

"How do you know?"

I had to think, how did I know? "Okay, an old man, on Miz Audrey's block, died this summer and the ambulance was there most of the morning. I left early that day and it was still there at one."

"Oh." Jan sat back. Maybe thinking about what we'd said, maybe believing Penny was still alive.

Jose entered the freeway, marked 92 toll entrance, I looked at the bridge, concrete with traffic in both directions on one level.

"I can't do this, Jose."

"Yes, you can. Close your eyes, don't look," Then he whispered to Jan, "she's afraid of bridges, I should have taken the Bay Bridge."

"Hey, I'm scared, not deaf!"

"Since when are you afraid of bridges?"

"Since we crossed one earlier."

"Go figure."

The water was right there, on either side of us. It looked close enough to touch, It was dirty and looked cold,

"Folks be out here crossing these bridges every day?" I asked.

Jan and Jose laughed. "Yeah, chile, they be out here doin' just that," Jan said, and they laughed again.

That embarrassed me. God knows, I know how to talk, but it just doesn't come to me naturally. I can say anything I need to say in perfect English, if I could just remember to think about it first. I wondered if that's what it's like for the true "English as a second language" people.

"Don't you be back there brooding, hard as you are on me about my stuff. You know I love you. And looking at this young man when he looks at you, I believe he thinks he'd be licking sugar if he got a few laps off your face."

Poor Jose, now Jan Channey was up there embarrassing him too.

"Shut up, Jan Channey. You got stuff to be thinking about."

"Point made."

"I'll listen next time you say you're off pork, that makes you crazy," I mumbled to myself for all to hear.

I could see her smile and I wasn't even facing her. She let her head fall back on the head rest. I couldn't see it, but I imagine she closed her eyes. I looked ahead. At least Jan's silliness had taken my mind off the bridge and we were more than half way across it. I buried my head in the clean-smelling vinyl.

"Are you okay back there?" Jose asked.

"Fine," I mumbled, the word bouncing off the seat and back into my face. He was talking to me, a good sign, Jan hadn't embarrassed him into silence.

I was surprised to find myself waking up when the car stopped moving, I didn't even know I was sleepy. I'm beginning to suspect I sleep when I'm afraid.

"Where are we?" I looked around. We were in a decent enough neighborhood, mostly apartments. Not enough houses and too many cars parked around to call it a nice neighborhood, but decent.

"This is where I live, Tennessee. We figured you and Jan could hide out here while we set up the trap."

We decided, I repeated his words in my mind, I wondered what that meant. Was Jan trying to set me up with this kid or was she working her own plan? Probably not the latter, I decided, who has time to thank about such things when somebody's trying to kill them?

Jose pulled up to the back of a large brown building. The building was three stories high and, depending on their sizes, it looked like it could have housed fifteen or sixteen apartments.

Jose got out first and looked all around. It finally dawned on me, Jose was playing I-Spy. Come Monday when his coworkers ask, "how did you spend your long weekend, Jose?" boyfriend was going to have an answer for them,

He opened the door and leaned in. "The coast is clear."

Jan opened her door and started out before I had a chance to tell her my observation,

All of the apartments opened up on an outside terrace, so Jose didn't have a chance to canvas a hallway for us.

His apartment was a surprise. I expected, what? A young man's apartment, mixed-matched furniture, makeshift bookcases, that kind of thing.

The room we stepped into was big, bright and airy. There

were off-white drapes hanging neatly at the large picture window, an entertainment center loaded with a television and a bunch of black boxes with silver dials that probably made-up his "system."

"This is nice," Jan said, making herself comfortable on his plaid sofa, "I know you didn't think to put that tablecloth on that table. What woman helped?" She pointed to his dining area. There was a round table with a frilly navy table cloth and a vase of silk flowers in the center,

"See, that's sexist. Why do you assume I needed a woman's hand in my decorating?"

"Did you need a woman's hand?" Jan asked.

Jose grinned. "No, I did it all by myself. That's my story and I'm sticking to it." He walked to the kitchen, all visible from the recliner I'd chosen to sit on, and took three glasses from the cabinet. "I know you ladies like diet sodas, but all I have is plain old cola,"

"Now who's being sexist?" Jan asked. She was remarkably cool, but that's Jan Channey for you. Even when we were young adults, her problems were just about over at the point she said them aloud, mine just feel worst mixed with oxygen.

Jose returned to the room carrying glasses of colas and, bless his heart, coasters for our glasses. He sat next to Jan.

"Okay, Ladies, what's the plan?" he asked, with an I-Spy grin all over his cutie-pie face.

I had a plan, maybe not much of a plan, but the only one among the three of us. It would require some help. I wanted Jan to ask Medicine Man to help us,

"There must be another way," she said,

"Okay, you tell me, what is it?"

"I don't know."

"Are you sure it's not them?" Jose asked.

"Pretty sure,"

"Then they seem perfect for the job. I could pretend to offer the help of my friends, but I wouldn't want them to get involved and I wouldn't let them come in without knowing the risks."

"No, we can't involve anybody else. It needs to be the Shivs," I said.

"I'll owe them if they do it." I could see the idea of being indebted to the gang scared her.

Then something occurred to me. "So what, you'll be in Tennessee."

"If I make it out of this, I better be elsewhere."

"Then you'll call?"

"I'll call."

Jose stood. I didn't know why until he left the room and returned with a cordless telephone. He handed it to Jan.

"Do you know the number?" I asked.

"Numbers R Me," was all she said as she punched the buttons. "Man there?" she asked, in a tough street voice I'd heard her use before. "Tell him it's Jan Channey, he'll know why."

I saw her tear a corner off of a magazine on Jose's cocktail table. Jose and I watched as she cradled the telephone on her shoulder and carefully folded the piece of paper until she made a tiny folded-over triangle. She looked up at that point and announced, "I'm on hold." Then she used the triangle to pick at her bottom teeth, "Bacon," she explained to me.

That was when I decided to distract Jose. I knew any minute Jan would locate the bacon bit that was annoying her and flick it across the room. I just didn't want Jose to have that image burned into his young mind.

"Show me the rest of your apartment," I asked.

"Okay." He stood and I copied. "It's just the one bedroom and the bathroom left."

By the time he finished saying that, we were standing in front of his neat little blue bathroom.

"I'm beginning to suspect blue is your favorite color."

"It is, blue like water, but I like all shades."

I could hear Jan from the living room, finally talking again. She was repeating the words, "okay, okay, got it," and it reminded me of the boys sitting at the table in Medicine Man's house.

"This is my bedroom. This is where I spend most of my time. I have that big TV in the living room and I end up in here watching that little thing. One of my boys ran the cable in here and I've got two speakers back here too,"

His room wasn't what I expected either. After seeing his nice living room, I expected a king-sized bed with a fake animal skin cover, something very masculine. He had a simple four poster full-sized bed and a simple blue chenille bedspread. There was a bookcase in there, loaded with books, and a small pine wood student's desk. His little television was on the single nightstand next to his bed.

The focal point of the room was a large wall painting that hung over his bed. She was probably the most wonderful painting I'd ever seen. "Now I know what people mean when they say somebody is striking," I told him.

Her skin was a half shade darker than mine. She was completely surrounded by a white satiny material, the contrast making her skin look like whipped chocolate. To say she looked like an angel just wasn't enough, but it was as close as I could come.

"This must be Monique?"

"No, she's not, but that's why I bought it. She could be Monique's sister. The artist, Michael Partee, is from out your way, Memphis."

I made a mental note to look up his work when I got home."This is nice, Jose. The whole apartment is very nice."

"Thanks, I spend a lot of time here. I like order."

"I can see that. But you saying that makes me wonder why you got involved with me and my mess?"

He sat on the corner of his bed, I sat at his desk.

"Brothers get a bad rap. Everywhere you look, on talk shows, newsstands, and book selves there something about the so-called division between the brothers and the sisters. I just know it's not true. I've sat up half the night listening to my friends talking about some sister who'd dogged them. When this is all over, I want you and Jan to tell your friends that a brother helped you—with no strings attached."

"Darling you can count on me to spread the word from here to Tennessee."

"Thanks."

"I guess we better get back in there and see if Jan's made any progress."

The young man actually held out his hand to me as I rose from the chair. If I was just ten years younger, I told myself, goodby Raymond, hello Jose.

Jan was sitting at the dining table when we got back. She was staring at the telephone like it was a television set.

"What are you doing?" I asked,

"I started telling Man the plan and he stopped me. He said somebody would call me back here in ten minutes with another number for me to call."

"Wow," Jose said. "Somehow you just don't expect petty neighborhood thugs to be that organized."

"No, you don't, and that's why I don't want to be beholden to them."

All three of us nodded in agreement.

FOURTEEN
♠

The plan had to be altered. Jose discovered the flaw in it.

"If you're so sure the Shivs aren't involved, then you can't stay here tonight," he told me, soon after Jan had completed her call to Man's "safe" number.

"Why?" we both asked.

"You have to do everything you had planned to do when you left Jan's mother's house. Everything you told them you were going to do."

I saw Jan Channey flinch. It would have been hard for me to accept that somebody in my family wanted me dead too. Although the thought of killing Emerald is one of my frequent fantasies.

Judging by his next statement, Jose saw her reaction too.

"If it's not the Shivs, then whoever it is has a close connection to the comings and goings at your mother's house," he said, this time facing Jan. "From what you told me." He faced me. "Everybody expected you to come back, probably, even Mother Stovall. You've got to go back and act like nothing has changed,"

We all nodded. He was right. But I didn't want to go back there. I felt comfortable in Jose's apartment. I felt safe. I was beginning to question my own bright idea.

"What time is it?" Jan asked.

"Almost seven, we've got a shaky two hours of daylight left."

"So I better get going?"

"So you better get going," we agreed.

We didn't waste a whole lot of time talking about it after that. Within minutes, Jose and I were in his car. My stomach made a loud embarrassing growl, just before he popped in a tape, when the car was silent and even the lack of traffic noise was working against me. I'm sure there are poor, pitiful, dirty, old men, drunk, living in cardboard boxes whose stomachs don't make such noises. I knew I should say something, there was a possibility he could have thought I was passing gas.

"I guess you're hungry too?" he asked, saving me the trouble of thinking up something to say.

"What would give you that idea?" I asked, using Jan's sweet innocent's voice.

He laughed. "I know a place near here that makes burritos to die for. How does that sound?"

I'm not really adventurous when it comes to food. I've had burritos before, but I'm a collard greens and cornbread kind of sister. I looked at Jose, he wasn't waiting for an answer.

The dinner menu was decided.

The restaurant with the "burritos to die for" was a small greasy neighbor storefront; the kind of place that you know must have good food or nobody would risk eating there. Jose pulled into a spot a new Cadillac was leaving.

"This shouldn't take long," he said, opening his door.

"Wait!" I shouted. I don't know why it was a shout, it just came out that way. "Use this," I handed him a fifty.

He glanced at the rear view mirror and closed the door.

"Put that away, Ruby. I wouldn't make it back to the car flashing around fifties in that place."

"This is on me I told you before . . . "

He smiled and threw up his hand in my face like a crossing guard saying stop. My experience with my trying-to-act-young sister let me know what he was saying. Whenever Emerald does the hand thing she says, "talk to the hand, I'm not listening."

"Okay, Jose, go get your 'to die for burritos.'"

He checked the mirror again and jumped out when the traffic cleared. I could see his progress in the line from the car. If lines are any kind of indication, the burritos probably were good. I tried to get my mind ready. Like I said, I'm not an adventurous eater. Mexican food should be eaten by Mexicans and I couldn't see anybody, other than Jose, who looked like what I believed a Mexican should look like. That started me wondering, if it's so good, where's the Mexicans?

Emerald likes to eat, I could have stopped my thought there, but what I was remembering was Emerald likes to eat all kinds of exotic food. We try to eat out once a month. Sometimes we'll ask our parents or Aunt Vivian to join us, but even if we don't we eat out the first Friday of the month. It's right after she gets her check and I get paid every Friday. On the Fridays I get to choose, we eat at Puff's House of Ribs or one of the three fast food chicken places in town. When I had my car, Emerald has taken us as far as Memphis to sample dishes can't neither one of us pronounce. I just hate discovery eating, I take my food seriously. But one time we went to a Chinese restaurant and she got up almost as soon as we sat down.

"Where are you going?" I asked her.

"I just glanced into the kitchen when that waiter came out."

I stood too. "It was dirty, huh?" I asked, while I was slipping my jacket back on.

"It was okay, but all I saw were white folks and a black man back there."

I waited for her to say more, but apparently, she thought she was finished. "So what, Emerald?"

" Huh? "

"So what you saw white folks and a brother back there?"

"Shoot, Girl, I ain't paying for no Chinese food that wasn't cooked by a China man or woman. And look around the room."

Her head swiveled around and I did the same.

"Where's the Chinese people? If they don't eat here, there's a reason."

It didn't seem like a good time to point out that there is no Chinese population in Petite to speak of. I understood her point.

I glanced at the line, Jose was next.

The car immediately took on the smell of burritos when he returned.

"I figured we'll eat them in the car," he said, and then he surprised me by pulling away from the curb. We drove for about five minutes before we were back in front of Lake Merritt. There weren't as many people around, a few joggers, several pairs of lovers, two boy-girl combinations and one boy-boy. I had to remind myself I was in California. Before I made that reminder, I was imagining the shorter boy was just some very strange looking girl who was fortunate enough to have found a very attractive boy who wanted to hold her hand in public.

"Remember what we were saying about using the daylight."

I felt I had to say something, Jose had let his seat back and was dispensing burritos like he planned to spend the night.

"I know, just as long as it takes for us to eat them. Promise."

He placed the bag with mine in it on my lap,

I watched as he unwrapped his burrito. It was big, I can say that for it. He broke a third of his off, it looked like I saw rice, beans, meat and a thick oozing white sauce tinged in red. It was, in the words of my niece, Pearl, gross-looking big time.

I watched him open those full perfect lips and engulf the whole third. He moaned as he started chewing. Shoot, I didn't feel like I should eat mine. The way he was acting, I figured I should take it back to Tennessee with me and enclose it under glass. The way those silly women down there be hanging up perfectly fine quilts on their walls and be freezing under little flimsy store bought spreads.

"Eat, Tennessee."

"But I'm enjoying watching you so much,"

"Watching me is not going to stop your stomach from growling."

He was right, but it was no telling what kind of sounds would be coming out of me after eating something with beans, rice and cheese in it. I opened mine and bit off a small bite. I got a mouthful of bread or tortilla or whatever it's called. I tried a second mouthful. It was messy, but tasty. I couldn't see myself laying down my life for one, but I could probably finish half.

"Do you like it?"

"It's good," I half-heartedly mumbled with a full mouth.

"Oh, Tennessee, don't tell me you don't like Mexican. Don't tell there's one thing that makes us not perfect for each other."

I waited until I stopped chewing. Actually the shell was the thing stopping me from giving it two thumbs up. It was a little too chewy, almost rubbery.

"You better stop messing with me, child. You can't toy with an old woman's emotions—don't you know that?"

"When I meet one, I'll remember."

We finished our burritos, he finished his and I ate a little more then half of mine. "Are you ready for this, Ruby?"

"As ready as I'm going to get."

"It's not too late for us to bring the police in. You know, regardless of what Jan says, they have to help—that's their job."

He really was young to believe that. I had to go with Jan on the police matter. Sure they would come, in time to draw a chalk outline around her body. No, this was something Jan would have to do herself, with a little help from her friends.

When we pulled up in front of Jan's mother's house, Mother Stovall was sitting in a lawn chair in front of her closed garage door. She openly watched us as I had a few departing words with Jose and then got up and headed inside just as I started my approach to the Channey front door. It looked like she moved to keep from speaking to me, but my paranoia said she could have needed to make a call about me too.

"I was starting to get worried about you," Mrs. Channey said, as she unlatched the screen door. It was still warm out, but starting to cool a bit.

I don't know if it was because it was later in the day or because I knew there was a problem, but this time I could smell the rum as soon as I entered the house. She leaned in like she was going to kiss my cheek. "Is my baby all right?" she whispered.

I glanced around the room. There were noises in two different directions, but we were the only people visible.

"She's fine," I said.

"Come in, sweetie. Tell me what you think of California so far."

That threw me, she was acting like I just returned from Disneyland. I ruled out Mrs. Channey, although until I did it, I hadn't realized she was on my list. "Who's home?" I asked.

"Everybody. Pam's in the kitchen and I believe Glenn's in his room on the telephone."

"Where's Dante?"

She looked at me like she's forgotten her son-in-law's name or maybe that he lived there too. "Come to think about it, I haven't seen him since before Oprah went off." Then she did exactly what I would have not wanted her to do. "Pam, Pam," she hollered,

Pam appeared immediately, actually fast enough to have been listening to us near the door. Paranoia again?

"Hi, Ruby, you're back. I hope you found that all is well wherever you went?" She tried to sound casual, but it was obvious she knew I'd been visiting Jan.

I glanced at Mrs, Channey and she looked away. Clearly this wasn't a woman who could keep secrets.

"Where's Dante?" her mother asked. Pam flashed a look at me, jealousy or concern that I could suspect her husband of something? I couldn't tell.

"Dante's mother called. She needed him to pick up a prescription for her. Why do you ask, Mama?"

"I haven't seen him for a while, just asking."

Pam looked at me again and then back at her mother.

"He hasn't been gone that long. I imagine he'll be back any minute. Although his mother does have a tendency to find all kinds of things for him to do once she gets him over there. He's such a good son."

"Humph," Mrs. Channey grunted. Anger rose in Pam's cheeks.

"Mama," Pam started, but she knew there was nothing she could say. She looked like she was going to cry. Mrs, Channey waved off her daughter and returned to her chair.

I needed an exit, "I think I got off on the wrong foot with your neighbor, Mother Stovall, this afternoon. I think I'll go over and apologize."

"Who gives a shit?" Mrs. Channey said,

"Mother!" Pam commented, but then she turned to me.

"In her own crude way, Ruby, Mama's right. We don't care about what you said to Mrs. Stovall. As far as I'm concerned you can go over there and gangster slap her a few times for me."

"I know, but she is an older woman and I wouldn't want anybody to disrespect my mother."

"I understand. Jan always said you're a real sweetheart."

"Some folks don't deserve the respect you'd give a damn dog, Thaddie Stovall is one of those people," Mrs. Channey said.

She picked up her glass and took a nice long drink. Then she repositioned herself to face the television screen. School was out, I could leave.

"When you get back you can eat, if you're ready," Pam said, again smiling a sweet little sister smile.

Was this girl's elevator making it to the top?

"Okay," I agreed, to speed up my departure. But I knew I wouldn't want to eat again so soon.

Mother Stovall was sitting in front of the garage again.

"Well, look what the cat dragged back. I wondered how long it would take for you to get back over here."

She must have been expecting me or somebody else, there was a second lawn chair out. "You knew I was coming, is that what you're saying?" I asked, smiling. I was determined not to let this old woman get to me.

"Yeah, I knew. Sooner or later everybody makes their way to Mother Stovall. You want to know who's over there trying to kill that little Channey slut."

FIFTEEN

♠

You could have pushed my fat ass over with a feather. I have a poker face I can rely on—when I'm playing poker or *expecting* a zinger. But I was sure Mother Stovall was able to read every thought and emotion that flashed through my body. My first reaction? Bitch! How dare you call my friend a slut? She doesn't sleep with married men, especially not with their families right next door.

"Now are you going to sit back and have an intelligent conversation with me or just sit there with your nostrils opening and closing like a crack house door?"

"Mother Stovall, I'm a good southern daughter. I've been raised to respect older people, whether they deserve it or not. But make no mistake about it, I know how to get a body told and I'm not going to sit here and let you call my best friend too many more sluts without telling you what I know about your past."

Thaddie Stovall threw her head back and laughed, actually cackled like they say old folks do. I saw all seven teeth in the top of her mouth.

"You go girl," she said, adding insult to insult. This woman needed to see the back of somebody's hand seconds before it slapped the smile off her rose red penciled and painted lips. Still grinning she added, "I tell you what, I won't call your little friend names and you can keep whatever you *think* you know about me to yourself. Now let's talk about the real issues."

That was my only reason for wasting daylight with her, but she sat back and crossed her arms. She was going to make me ask her for whatever she thought she had.

"What do you know Mrs. Stovall?"

"Mother."

"Mother Stovall."

"I know the Channey's are as dysfunctional as any family ever sat up on Oprah's stage." She smiled, proud of herself for coming up with a word like dysfunctional.

"Show me a family that's not and I'll show you a pack of dysfunctional liars. Give me some information I can use."

"What have you got for me?"

"What do you want?"

She seemed to be thinking about my question. I hadn't expected to buy any information, I wondered how much it would cost.

"Can you get an apology for me from that Channey woman? I never slept with Big Luther. Some folks think men and women can't be friends."

Damn, this woman was full of surprises. Money, which was an impossibility, would be easier to get than an apology from Mrs. Channey. I was fairly certain of that.

"Not a snowball's chance in hell,"

"That's what I thought." The realization seemed to disappoint her.

"This isn't about Mrs. Channey, it's about Jan. What has she ever done to you?"

"Nothing. Actually, I liked Jan and Pam when they were little girls. They used to visit. They'd bring me their reports cards and I'd give them a quarter for every "A." They didn't get their mother's ugly ways until just recently. Walking past, not speaking. What kind of upbringing is that? As many trips as Pam makes to the Safeway, you'd think she'd stop by and ask, 'Mother Stovall, can I get something for you?' She can find the time to visit that brother-in-law of hers. You'd think she'd offer me a trip or two to Safeway. You'd think that wouldn't you?"

"Yes, ma'am."

"Indeed. Wasting all her time kissing up to that big-lipped sucker she's married to, that's her problem."

"Dante?"

"If that's what his name is. Knowing his family, he could have several, and some numbers instead of names too."

I wasn't tracking this at all. "Several what, families?"

She looked at me in that way old women and teachers have, designed to make the lookee feel stupid, "Girl, where did you say you were from?"

No, she was not going to start in on me about my hometown. "Why?" I asked, "you planning a vacation?"

She snorted and ignored the question. "That boy Dan-te, ain't nothing but trouble, just like his brothers up there in Folsom. And don't think that mother-in-law of his doesn't know it. Big Luther knew it. He knew those Luckenbills."

"Why don't you tell me about them." I made a mental note to find out what Folsom was.

"It's not just a crime, it's a sin—what they did to that beautiful house. See that's why they don't want us up there anyway, a few like them. They're garbage. They spoil it for the rest of us."

"Ma'am, I don't know what you're talking about." Up where, in Folsom?

"I know you don't know and that's why that child is as good as dead."

I took a deep breath. I'd already discovered Ruby Gordon's mind wasn't going to figure this out. I tried to think like Miz Audrey.

"Okay," I said, "let me work this out aloud." Miz Audrey says that sometimes too; then she starts listing off everything I just told her until something clicks in her mind. "Dante and his family are garbage, this is well known?"

Thaddie Stovall nodded.

"It's a sin what they did to that house. Are we talking about the Channey's house?"

Thaddie Stovall gave a look of disappointment before she

shook her head.

"Another house?"

Thaddie Stovall nodded,

"House, house." I wasn't getting anything. Something clicked or so I thought, "The Shivs, what they did to that house!" The paint job had to be some kind of minor sin.

She stood up, slowly but deliberately. "I'm going in if you're going to be stupid."

"No, please, sit down. This is important. If you're not willing to tell me what I need to save my friend's life, give me a chance to guess it." If I sounded like I was begging, I was.

"Look, Girl, don't you go around telling nobody that I told you anything." She sat back down.

"Yes, Ma'am."

"Don't you bring those Shivs on me. They ain't got a damn thing to do with it!"

"How can you be so sure?"

"All I got is some old woman's theories—you understand?"

"Yes, Ma'am,"

"Now I got things to do, people to see. I'm going to tell you one more thing. Figure out who's got the most to gain and why they need that gain. Then you'll know who's shooting up that house." She stood, grabbed her chair and spoke over her shoulder, "Bring my other chair to the door."

I did as she instructed. When I got to the door, I peeked inside and saw a clean house, with a dining room table set for two with candles in the holders and wine chilling. Mother Stovall was expecting a gentleman caller.

"Since I like you I'll give you a bonus. Find out why they sent my sweetie Rasan away."

"Rasan," I repeated. I should say I repeated to a closed door because Mother Stovall had shut the door in my face.

♣♣♣

Mrs. Channey hadn't moved since I left.

"Didn't know a damn thing, did she?" she asked, not looking away from the television.

"Not really."

"I could have told you that. She wants to be a power broker in the neighborhood, but she doesn't go anywhere—how she gonna know anything?"

I had a feeling the news came to Mother Stovall and she was smart enough to make a story out of it, but I didn't say this to Mrs. Channey. I sat down opposite her.

"I'd like to talk to Rasan. He's my godson, I'd hate to come this far and not see him."

"You can't."

"I can't talk to him?"

"Nope." She was watching a woman getting liposuction on a news show. Her body was jerking with each plunge of that suction stick into the woman's belly. "You ask me, that's worth the pain and cost. If I ever hit the lottery, I'm going to find me somebody to suck out these thighs. I'll show you pictures. In my day, I was never this big."

"Yes, Ma'am," Why were we talking about this? I wanted her to explain to me why I couldn't see Rasan, "Mrs. Channey, about Rasan. Why can't I see him?"

"He's gone already."

"Gone where?"

She looked up at the clock, "They should have left two hours ago. He's with a group of them going on a bus trip this weekend. Pam, Pam!"

Pam appeared from the kitchen again. "Where's Rasan going on that bus again?"

"To visit some of the traditionally black colleges." Her tone was one of annoyance. Apparently this was a question her mother had asked before. Pam looked at me. "Rasan's other grandparents have him in a group that helps kids get ready for college. They'll visit six campuses before they get back Tuesday morning."

"Oh, sounds like a good group."

Pam left the room again, this time heading in the direction of the bedrooms. "Mrs. Channey, why did Rasan move in with his other grandparents?"

"They were always trying to get him to come over there. They do have a nice big house and they're good people. Now, Milton will go in his garage and smoke that dope. He says it's for his glaucoma, but his eyes look fine to me. I ain't never even seen him squint, but it's okay, they're good people. It couldn't be any worst than the little taste I take now and then."

Little taste my ass. "But why let Rasan move in with them now?"

"We figured it was best to separate him and Dante, before somebody got hurt. I'm too old to be separating big grown men, you know that?"

I nodded. I figured it was best to nod and let her talk.

"See, Rasan is serious when it comes to his mother."

They were showing the six weeks after picture of the liposuctioned woman. Mrs. Channey grinned like she had a role in the procedure.

"Don't let me fool around and hit that lottery, yes, indeed." She sat back, pleased with herself. Some kind of pseudo postsurgical joy?

I checked the clock. The telephone call for me was scheduled to come through in less than ten minutes and I could still hear Glenn talking on it, I wondered if they had call waiting.

"Is Glenn planning to go out tonight?" I asked.

"Probably, these women nowadays are like leeches. Once they get in their heads that a boy is good marriage material they won't let go."

"I was hoping I could talk to him again'"

Without warning, she screamed out, "Glenn!" That was when I saw what had struck me as strange about her call-outs. Most people will turn their heads in the direction of the person they're calling to. Mrs. Channey just screams, never taking her eyes off the television screen.

In the next few minutes Glenn came out. "You're back, huh?

Couldn't pass up the chance to spend the night listening to her snoring," he said smiling, and nodding his head at his grandmother. She was watching one of those most wanted programs now. He went behind her chair and started massaging her neck and shoulders. Looked like he was doing a good job too. I wondered if he did non-family,

When I saw him earlier, he was dressed in a blue jumpsuit with his name on it. Now he was dressed in a pair of dark tan pants and tan print shirt and a tie. He wasn't as stocky as I thought, in fact, I didn't see anything wrong with his body.

"I was hoping we could talk again,"

"I was getting ready to eat, but you're welcome to join me." He leaned down and kissed his grandmother on the cheek in a manner that told me he wasn't thinking about it, it was something he did naturally and often. She patted his hand, never once looking away from the screen.

I was surprised to see Glenn's plate when he exited the kitchen and sat down to join me at the dining room table. There were two pieces of cornmeal-coated, hard-fried fish on his plate with rice and green beans, but it was the fish that interested me, I hadn't smelled it cooking. I thought it odd that Pam could have been back in the kitchen frying fish without the smell reaching the living room. The house wasn't that big. That's just me obsessing (Miz Audrey's word) about something that ain't got nothing to do with anything,

"You sure you don't want to eat, Aunt Pam can put her foot in some fish?"

"Yeah, it looks good, but I just had a burrito to die for."

I guess I shouldn't have been surprised when he called the name of the burrito place. This was his home. I let him talk a little about himself, men like to do that. He told me about his job as a machine operator in a small factory and the classes he was taking at the community college. I watched his hands as he spoke, big working man hands. I've got a weakness for blue collar hands. The only thing a manicured man's finger can do for me is point me in the direction of a hard-working man. Poor Raymond can't get finished cutting my lawn if I sit out back and watch him. As soon as his face get a light sweat on it, I'm calling him in to take care of more pressing business.

"You're not listening to me."

"What?" I had zoned out on his hands.

"If you were listening and heard what I just said, you would be slapping my face right now," He was grinning, his big brown eyes flashing like Jan Channey's when she's flirting with some unsuspecting sap.

"What did you say, Glenn?"

"I like the way you say Gla-enn, like it's two syllables."

"Okay, now you're going to make fun of my accent too. But don't forget this is Oakland, home of Ebonics."

"I just said I liked it, if I wanted to make fun of it, I would have chosen some different words. You don't listen when you're listening either."

When he said that something clicked in my head. 'You don't listen when you're listening,' I mentally repeated. Pam had told me something about, what? If I could remember where we were at the time. Not the kitchen, in her mother's room sitting on the bed. She had asked me to tell Dante to come to her and he went to the bedroom. Mrs. Channey took me back out back while they were in the bedroom. Now all I had to remember was what she said and why it was trying so hard to push through the normal haze in my mind.

"So you're welcome to come along if you like."

Glenn was waiting for me to answer him. He'd asked if I wanted to tag along with him and his date; to see a bit of the Oakland night life.

"No, thanks. I've probably seen as much of any city's night life as I ever need to see."

"Now you sounding like Aunt Jan. Come on, it's not over until you say it's over."

"Dar-ling, it's over. My partying days are too far behind me to look back and pull them forward. And, I really don't miss them enough to care."

"Why is that? I've heard other people not that much older than me saying that. How do you know?"

125

"When it all starts looking the same. And every man, or woman in your case, sounds like the one before her. And the thought of taking a shower and getting dressed is too exhausting. Then you know it's time to give it up."

"It won't happen, I live for the weekend."

"It'll happen."

"Bet."

"You're on."

Of course there'd be no way to collect on such a silly bet, but I did enjoy shaking that big working man's hand.

SIXTEEN
♠

I asked Glenn about Rasan and he started to tell me
something, something that made him glance around the room first,
something that made him sit very still to see if he could hear anybody
nearby.

He placed his fork on the plate and wiped his face with the
blue napkin. He crunched the napkin in an angry ball and looked
around again,

"Dante and Rasan couldn't get along. Dante has a way
of fuc . . . excuse me, messing with people; without even trying. He
wanted to father Rasan. You know, give him advice and expect the
boy to follow it. You can't wait until a boy's damn-near grown and
start that. And Dante's advice wasn't really anything the boy needed
to hear anyway. He'd tell him stupid shit, excuse me, but you know
what I mean,"

"Like what?"

"Rasan has a girlfriend, He's devoted to this little girl and
she's a nice person—good for him. Dante was constantly telling him
he was too young to get tied down. Kept telling him, he should 'run
the hoes.' Of course Rasan's got too much sense to listen to that

foolishness. Certainly not while they're always saying how high the AIDS stats are for this area. And I wouldn't be surprised if Dante didn't try to hit on Adina, that's her name. Rasan doesn't bring her around any more."

I nodded.

"Plus, Dante got a thing about Jan."

"What do you mean?"

"They don't get along. I didn't think too much about it at first, I figured he had the hots for her. Since he couldn't act on them, I figured he just messed with her out of frustration. It might still be that, but I'm sure Rasan wouldn't see it that way."

"What kind of person is he?"

"What do you mean?"

I never got a chance to tell him what I meant or to hear his answer. In the next second Dante came through the front door and the telephone rang. Dante was already en route so he answered it.

"Yeah, she's here. Who's this I can barely hear you?"

When I heard Dante say that, I thought it was somebody else, not the call I was expecting.

He looked at me while he listened, but I didn't know how to interpret it. Finally he lower the receiver, put his hand over the mouthpiece and spoke directly to me. "Some woman's on the phone, wants to talk to you. She claims her name is P. Bessie Burns."

I resisted the urge to smile. It's a name from our college days, Jan Channey called Project Bootstrap, Bessie when somebody was near she didn't want to say Project B.S. around.

Dante wasn't buying it and he wasn't supposed to. I took the telephone and dragged the long cord back to the dining room with me. Glenn had gone; he'd put his plate in the kitchen and was back in the bedroom.

"Hello, Bessie." I listened while Jan told me all was going as planned. "Sure I can do that, no problem. Okay, bye."

When I turned around, Dante and Mrs. Channey were looking right in my mouth. "What time is it?" I asked, as if they had a right to listen in on my calls. They both just stood there, unable to compute my words. What did the time have to do with a call from somebody calling herself Bessie? Mrs. Channey actually shook her head, like they

128

do on television when they're trying to clear their thoughts. She looked at the little travel clock.

"It's a quarter after seven. Why?"

"I'm going out for a while . . . I'm going for a walk."

Both of them repeated, "a walk," like I said I was going to fly across the bay wearing a pair of wax wings.

"That's right, I'm a walker. In fact, when we were in college, Jan and I probably walked that whole town a couple of times."

"That's my little Jan all right, she's a walker." Mrs. Channey was already distracted, but Dante wasn't buying it.

"This ain't no place for a stranger to be out walking."

"I went out walking this afternoon, so I'm not a stranger anymore." Smiling, I added, "any way, you don't have to worry about me, I'm strapped." I was thinking about the umbrella "weapon" Mrs. Channey had given me earlier and I had stored in my big leather purse. I called myself making a joke.

"I heard that," he commented.

I started to tell him what I was kidding about, but then thought, 'why bother.'

Glenn was coming out of the bedroom with his jacket and we met at the door.

"Did you change your mind about going out with me, us?"

"No, I'm just going for a walk,"

"A walk! Why?"

"I like to walk."

He didn't speak again until we were on the sidewalk. "You be careful, Ms. Ruby. I ain't going to tell another adult how to conduct her business, but I wouldn't be out here walking."

"I'll be okay," I said, as I started in the same direction I'd taken earlier to get to Medicine Man's house. I didn't hear the car door slam right away and I pictured him watching me walk away. I tried not to waddle.

SEVENTEEN
♠

It was that time of day when I find it difficult to drive. There was still enough sun out to make you believe you should be able to see whatever's out there, but the sun was fading fast enough to create shadows and floaters on an old girl's eyes. I was stepping carefully, remembering the uneven sidewalks and the cracks I'd seen earlier. I had my purse double-wrapped and hanging in the pit of my left arm, leaving my right arm free to hit anybody who thought he had a right to my stuff.

It was hard not to look back to see if I'd picked up a tail. Everybody in the house, except Pam knew I was out walking. I figured by now even Pam knew about the strange call from the alleged Bessie that had prompted me out for a "walk." I walked really slow past Mother Stovall's house. I even paused, from the sidewalk, and glanced into her big picture window. I saw two figures sitting at the dining room table. The candles were lit. I almost waved, but I figured that would have been overkill. I noticed a white Monte Carlo in the driveway with one of those metal panels on the driver's door. It read, Northern California Life. Mother Stovall was screwing the neighborhood insurance man; I wondered if he was somebody's husband too.

Kids were still out. Younger teen age boys and the little girls they attract, were playing basketball in the driveway of one of the nicer homes. They took no notice of me as I passed. The girls didn't even care enough to look me up and down and criticize my clothes or body. Damn, I thought, I must really be getting old.

Again, the thought that Glenn would be the person who would care enough to follow me ran across my mind. This time I wasn't able to push it out. I liked the man, I hoped he wasn't trying to kill his aunt and I couldn't begin to come up with a motive, but stranger things have happened. Stranger things have happened with me there to see them.

I rounded the corner that would put me on the street with the liquor store. As I turned, I was able to get a good look behind me. I didn't see Glenn's car, but I didn't see anybody else's that I recognized either. I saw a little figure coming into view near the telephone I'd used earlier. I knew it was Jan, but I hoped anybody behind me wouldn't know that because she was standing still. In the plan she was supposed to spend her time moving around in front of the busy store and circling the drunks she had, rightfully, predicted would be there. Spotting me, she started in my direction. It must have been instinctive, but she stopped herself before taking more then two or three steps. She ducked into the store and, before I was less than ten feet from the main door, she appeared again. I tried to find Jose's car. I didn't see it until I was directly in front of the store. It had been hidden by a van. When I was turning to enter the store, where Jan had retreated again, I noticed a silver Lexus parked across the wide street. Jose had a nice car, but it didn't stand out in this neighborhood with late modeled cars parked on the street behind clunkers. But the silver Lexus screamed, "look at me," and I had to look. There was a single man in the car, a dark-skinned brother wearing sunglasses that should have seriously impaired his vision. Something in the slow, easy, confident movement of his head as he bobbed it up ever so slightly as a greeting to me, told me that Medicine Man could see everything that was happening on the street—and possibly some things yet to happen.

The next few seconds were played out in slow motion, just like they show it in the movies. Jan called out my name. I assumed she hadn't seen Medicine Man and was about to ask me what or who was I nodding at. I began turning my head to face the store entrance again, my body was already turned mostly in that direction. I was smiling, I felt my smile drop as the next thing happened. A man who seemed to come out of the group of drunks barreled toward us from my left. His hand was extended, my first thought was that he was going for my purse. My eyes fell to his hand. I saw the gun.

Jan screamed

In the next second I heard two car doors slam.

Apparently, he heard it too. The man stopped liked he had been slapped, he had a thief's instincts. He turned and looked, first at Jose, and then his eyes bucked and I knew he'd seen Medicine Man crossing the street. He shoved the gun back into, where? It must have been a shirt pocket. The spot was too high for pants pocket. Jan fell to the floor near a magazine rack. It confused me because I knew I hadn't heard any shots. "Get up!" I screamed, but instead of getting up she slithered, with lightening speed, over to my feet and pulled me to my knees. I fell forward almost knocking over the rack. As I turned to catch myself with my right arm, I saw the man with the gun take a step and then jump into the brown van. The driver's side door was standing open for him. Somebody had been in the van.

Jose entered the store. He held out both hands to help us up at the same time. In the spit second it took to get back on the sidewalk, we saw the Lexus speeding away after the out-of-sight van.

"What now?" Jose asked, not really directing the question to either one us.

"I don't know," Jan answered, "I sure hope Man is able to catch him,"

We started to the car, I guess each of us not knowing what next, but knowing we didn't want to stand around the store. I glanced back at the opened store door and saw the Asian clerk on the telephone pointing at us. I wondered what the poor man thought had happened, I wondered if the police would come to check it out.

"The store clerk is calling the police," I announced as I held the front seat forward for her to get in the back.

"That bastard is probably putting in his second call. He made his first call when he looked up and saw three of us coming in."

Jose grinned, his first expression other than shock in ten minutes. I notice his right hand was shaking when he put the key in the ignition.

We didn't talk for the first five minutes in the car.
Jose didn't seem to have a destination in mind, he just drove.

"Let's go to our favorite place, Jose," I told him. He looked at me and smiled, I saw him, not little somebody's brother, but as a man. Like most men, he wanted to be in charge, but he didn't know what was suppose to happen. I'd given him something familiar—his favorite place by the lake. Apparently he was still thinking about it too. He reached over and took my left hand, he squeezed it.

"You're all right, Tennessee." He didn't linger with a long soulful look and let his hand drop to my thigh. He was saying, 'thanks for reminding me of a place that will take away my fear. Thanks for letting me be a man.'

I glanced back at Jan Channey. I knew she had to be out of it. My Jan Channey doesn't miss a thing. She would have seen Jose squeeze my hand. She would have said something sassy; something like, "coo-coo-a-chew, Mrs. Robinson." Something Jose would have been too young to understand. Something that would have tickled her into run away giggles even if nobody else in the car got it. The Jan Channey in the back had frightened herself into a ball so tiny she made the back seat look like full size.

"Did you see the gun Man was carrying?" Jose asked me. "I mean, just running down the street like that with a big ass semi automatic clearly visible."

I thought I heard admiration in his tone.

"I didn't see Medicine Man out of the car. But you do know how he's going to die? Don't you Jose?"

"What do you mean? How Medicine Man is going to die?"

"Right, he lives by the sword, he'll die by the sword."

"Yeah, that's probably true." There was a bit of sadness in his tone now.

I remembered the times I've gone to the movies with a mostly

133

black audience and some of the younger people cheered for the villains. I know a little about mental illness. Being black and young in this country can be a schizophrenic thing.

"He probably won't make it to your age."

"I wonder will it be worth it when his time comes. Maybe living fast and hard and dying young is the move. I don't know about you, but I'm not having a hell of a time in my responsible thirties."

"Yeah, well so far the forties haven't been much of a picnic either, but I've still got some hell left in me that I want to raise. So will you two get off this morbid track!" That was Jan Channey, back from wherever catatonic people go. "Tell us what you saw, Jose. I was in the store's doorway, what I remember doesn't make sense."

Jose looked out at his lake. He told us everything he remembered. I filled in the blanks where I could. The only new information, for me, was the order of Jose's and Medicine Man's rescue run. Jose said that he didn't know something was going down until he heard Man's car door slam. That means the second slam I heard was Jose's. So the man, with the gun, eyes must have bucked when he saw the semiautomatic.

"Did you get a better look this time, Jan?" I asked her.

"Do you know him?"

"No, but I have an even stronger sense that I've seen him somewhere before. But maybe not him some of his people or a picture, maybe." She snapped her fingers and repeated, "a picture." But then she shook her head. Whatever it was, it wasn't coming.

"Actually, I have a sense that I know him too."

"Maybe he went to college with you two?"

"No," we both said. There weren't that many black boys there and none of them could have grown up to be the man I saw.

"Maybe he's just one of those common-looking dudes," Jose offered.

"Maybe," I said, "but his image is burned in my memory now,"

"And probably Man's too. He's not a little brother you'd want to find yourself on the bad side of. Jose, maybe we better go over to the Shivs and find out what happened."

"If that's what you want." He leaned forward, about to turn the key.

"No, wait!" I was thinking while I was talking, "We can't go back there now. If Medicine Man caught up with the van and Jan's problems are over, is it a good idea for the third car involved in the liquor store incident to turn up outside of Man's house? No, I know where we need to go."

"Where?" they both asked.

"Back to Jan's mother's house. Somebody had to use the telephone or somebody left after me. When we find out who, we'll know who's trying to kill you."

Neither one of them commented. Which I assumed meant they agreed. We were pulling out of the parking spot when I heard a ringing telephone. The sound, though not loud, just about sent me through the roof of the car. "What is that?" I asked Jose.

"My cellular." He stopped the car, half in half out of its spot. "It's probably my mother. I've only had this thing for a month, she's the only one who seems to remember the number." As he was saying this, he was rooting around on the floor under his seat. There was another ring. He pulled up a black plastic case. I heard the Velcro pulling apart. "Hello," He listened. "No, I'm off this weekend." He listened. "Mama, can you call Sissy? I'm kind of busy right now." He listened. "No, it's not, I'm sure it's okay, call Sissy. Okay, I love you too. I'll stop by there tomorrow." He listened. "Actually, Mama, I've got two beautiful women with me right now." He listened. "Okay, I'll be careful. Bye." He put the little telephone back in its case and handed it to me. I guessed it was the co-pilot's job to put the telephone away. I placed it on the floor between us.

"She wants me to come over and take her blood pressure. She said my father has been in a funk all day and she believes he's caused her pressure to shoot up. What she really wants is for me to go over there and referee."

I wasn't interested in what his mother wanted. The only thing on my mind was the fact that he hadn't revealed he had a cellular. Why hadn't he given me that number before he'd gone to visit his aunt? I tried to remember if there were other times during the day when it would have made sense for him to say he had a telephone. I wondered what else he wasn't telling. I started replaying his role in all that had happened since my arrival. Who was Jose Montero? I needed to get Jan Channey by herself. We needed to talk.

EIGHTEEN
♠

They talked about the liquor store incident as we drove to Jan's house. She didn't seem to be acting any different with him, discussing strategies, speculating (Jose's word) about what happened if Man caught up with "the shootist" (Jan's word).

I couldn't comment. I didn't feel like I was among friends anymore. I guess I should say a friend, Jose was the only person I was doubting.

When we pulled up to Jan's mother's house, Jan said, "Uh-oh."

"What?" I asked.

"The house is dark. Our house is never dark, if nothing else we should be able to see the flicker of that damn television."

"Maybe they're in bed," Jose offered.

"No way. My mother catnaps in her chair all day so she can watch television most of the night."

Jose parked the car at the curb."Do you want me to go up to the door and check it out first?"

"No, if my family is laying in-wait, they won 't recognize you, I better go up alone."

137

Jan got out of the car, a lot easier then I could have gotten out. From behind she looked like she was dribbling a basketball up to the front steps. I guess her quick weaving and bobbing was designed to avoid bullets with her name on them. I saw her knock, wait, and then look around. She stood on her tiptoes and seemed to be taking off the porch light's globe.

She didn't take off the globe, but she did recover something, no doubt a key, because the next thing she did was open the door. We saw her disappear into the house and then reappear, beckoning from the door for us to come up.

"I guess the coast is clear," Jose said.

"Apparently,"

We got out and went into the house,

"This is too weird. They're all gone. Everything is just where they would have left it. It's like they just disappeared."

"Is there somebody we can call?" I asked.

"I can't think of anybody." She was perched on the arm of the sofa. Jose was sitting in Mrs. Channey's chair and I was pacing.

"Wait a minute, Glenn has one of those cellulars too. They're all the rage in Oakland." Jan was up again, moving toward the phone. I looked at Jose, thinking this conversation would spark some dialogue about his before unmentioned cellular.

Jose was looking at the TV Guide, he was on the crossword puzzle page. Jan dialed a number, waited a few seconds and dialed again."Glenn, this is Jan, I'm at Mama's and nobody's here." I expected her to say more, explain why that warranted a call, but apparently Glenn knew. I saw Jan listening intently. "Is he okay?" Her eyes stared at me, unblinking, unseeing, "You better be telling me everything. That's my baby you're talking about. You keep your telephone on you, I'll check back with you later. No, you can't reach me." Jan smiled, "She's going to be with me, why?" Jan pointed at me and smiled again. "We'll be around tomorrow. Maybe I can talk her into spending an extra night here, a fun night, Okay, Baby, bye now,"

"What's wrong?" I asked, sure something, albeit something minor, had happened to Rasan.

"Their bus was broadsided in Texas. Apparently one or two of the kids were shaken up and a few of the girls got dramatic and tried

138

to faint or some such, One of the parents called the Gibsons, Rasan's grandparents, and told them to expect a call from the hospital. They called my mother and she and Pam went over there to wait for the call. They called Glenn after Rasan called to tell them everything was fine."

"So what's next?" It was Jose's voice from behind us. Jan jumped as if she'd forgotten he was sitting there. She turned to face him.

"I don't know."

I feel like we should call Man and find out what happened."

"Do you know his number?" I asked.

"I have it in my room." She was already starting toward the back, I saw my opportunity.

"I need to get something too," I said, but it wasn't necessary, Jose was mentally doing the crossword puzzle.

NINETEEN
♠

"The way you're on my heels, you must have something to tell me. What is it?" Jan Channey asked, as soon as we entered her mother's room.

I didn't like the way she asked. There was attitude in her words, I started to tell her about herself then I realized she was probably feeling helpless, her son had been scared in a fender bender and she wasn't there to help him. Not to mention all the other shit. If there's one thing I know about a good sistha-girl, we get bull dog mad when we're feeling helpless,

"Don't start f-ing with me Jan Channey. I'll go out to that junior airport and wait for the next plane. I'll leave your little ass to the wolves." Yes, I understood what was happening in her head, but I was feeling helpless too, I wasn't going to let her get too deep in my big behind without fighting back. She looked me in the eyes and we both laughed.

"What do you want to say, Ruby?"

I sat on the bed and Jan joined me. I saw a flash of something out of the corner of my eye. It was so fast it was like I blinked and didn't realize it. Normally I wouldn't have noticed it, but I had a

140

problem with field mice getting into my house last year and I saw those flashes for about a month before I discovered the garage mice droppings. I decided to ignore it. It's not like we could stop and fight infestation too.

"Didn't you think it was odd that Jose had a telephone?"

"Huh? "

"A telephone. I meet this man, a good-looking man with nothing to do, and he agrees to take me around just for the pleasure of my company. We stop to use the phone, he calls me back to give me his aunts number—all when he has a telephone in the ride. You don't find any of this odd?"

She smiled and then popped me in the arm, which was totally unexpected. "I wondered when it would happen."

"What?"

"When you were going to find something wrong with Jose."

"What?"

"It happens every time. A man shows some interest in you and bam, something's wrong with him. When we were in college, Anson Avery . . . "

"That egg head pea hopper,"

"Lee Burton?"

"His breath smelled like old socks and raw potatoes."

"At least five different white boys

"Were white!"

"Were interested! And I know you couldn't care less about a person's race." She smiled and I knew she was remembering some of our white friends from Burns. "And poor Raymond?"

"What about Raymond?" I asked, sure I hadn't said anything bad about him.

"He's too old and boring. Or so you say."

"But I'm with him,"

"Have you given him your heart?"

"My heart's not up for grabs." I didn't want to have this conversation. Damn Jan Channey and her good memory.

"I didn't say did you let him grab it. I asked, have you given it to him?" she whispered, slow and carefully like she was talking to a limited child.

I didn't answer, I just looked at her, no doubt pouting, but so damn what?

"Okay, Ruby," she conceded. "But I'm telling you right now, if I make it out of this and we end up in Tennessee together, we're both getting husbands--by hook or by crook. I refuse to be like Mother Stovall waiting around for somebody else's husband to slip in and give me twenty minutes of affection twice a week." That triggered a thought, I tried to catch it; Mother Stovall, somebody else's husband,

"As far as Jose is concerned, I say we ask him. I think he's just a cute kid looking for a little excitement and possibly a mercy fuck. If he's a hit man how come he hasn't hit? Don't forget, I was alone with him for a couple of hours."

She was right, If he wanted to kill her he certainly had his opportunity. "You think he's shooting for a mercy . . . "

. We heard voices from the other room. Jan jumped up from the bed and cracked the bedroom door,

"I think it's Man," she whispered.

I remembered what I wanted to say about Mother Stovall,

"Mother Stovall is screwing the insurance man."

At first, Jan looked puzzled by my comment. "She is, huh? See, that's what I'm talking about, somebody else's husband."

"But . . . "

"Tell me later. I better get out there. My mother will have a fit, if she comes home and find Medicine Man in her house."

♠♠♠

I went to the living room and Jan went to the bathroom. She told me to go out and make sure Man didn't get too comfortable, she said she was under a lot of pressure to pee.

The men stopped talking when I entered. Man was standing by the door, Jose was standing a few feet from him.

I don't know how to stop a person from getting too comfortable. Neither one of them was sitting so I guess my job was done.

Man nodded at me and said, "Miss Ruby," as a greeting. Apparently the child had had some home training. He was wearing black leather pants and that little round African hat, in leather, that's so popular now. His shirt was one of those black and gray collarless deals. It was made out of some very expensive silk. The man looked *good*. Also, something about his look told me that he knew he favored Eddie and he knew how to play it,

Jan came running in with her jeans unzipped. She stopped in front of us, leaned back, making sure we all saw the tops of her lacy red devil panties and carefully (slowly) zipped her jeans. I wanted to laugh, I've seen her pull those kind of moves on guys a million times. She repeated them because they worked. Both men looked at her like she was made out of light rich milk chocolate and they were chocoholics.

"What've I missed?" she asked, like a virginal innocent. I could have beat her ass.

Jose looked up, but Man's focus was still at her crotch. It occurred to me that for somebody in such a hurry to get a hoodlum out of her mother's house, Jan had changed out of Penny's clothes and into some skin tight jeans and a lightweight sweater with a deep V neckline. I did laugh. They all looked at me and I got even more tickled.

"Ignore her," Jan said bobbing her head at me. "Come on and sit and tell me everything."

Old ass Jan Channey was making a play for Medicine Man. If time hadn't been an issue, I would have enjoyed watching it. She sat on the couch and patted the seat next to her while looking at Man. He grinned his Eddie Murphy grin and sat down. I sat on the other side of him and Jose got comfortable in the chair he had before. Jan tucked one foot under her and turned in to face Man. She touched his leather thigh and tapped it.

"Tell me," she said again, but before he could answer she rubbed his thigh. "This is some of the softest leather I've ever touched.

You need to quit, I said to her in my head.

143

"I bought these pants in Italy," Man said.

"Italy, wow, I haven't even been to Mexico."

I noticed she hadn't moved her hand. Thug or not, he was a child in the hands of a master.

"You like to travel?" he asked, thinking he was in control.

I looked over at Jose. He had that damn crossword puzzle in his face again.

"Did you catch the van?" I interrupted. They both snapped their heads and looked at me. "Excuse me." I said, I had to say something. Man looked a little angered by my question. He must have realized how he looked because his face softened, but not his eyes, "I know this man looks good enough to eat on a Ritz cracker, Jan Channey, but will you let him tell us what happened."

Jan rolled her eyes at me. Medicine Man smiled in earnest.

"There's really not much to say," he started looking first at me and then Jan. "I followed the van to Jack London Square. I lost him in traffic. But I'm pretty sure I saw the dude again, walking near one of the shops. If it was him, he's been inside."

Jan expression was as puzzled as mine,

"How do you know?" Jose asked.

"He walks like an ex-con. I don't know how to describe it. But I think it has something to do with walking around for years on those hard concrete floors."

Okay, so now we were looking for a familiar-faced ex-con. Maybe we've seen him on *Cops*, I thought. The idea tickled me again and I started laughing. Man turned to Jan and asked, "What countries would you like to visit?"

TWENTY
♠

"What do you call yourself doing with that child?" I asked, after Man had gone.

He'd been talking to Jan in a low intimate voice, virtually ignoring me and Jose. He'd casually checked his watch, looked slightly shocked for a few seconds, recovered, and made a cool slow exit like he had all the time in the world.

"Shh, he'll hear." Jan bobbed her head at Jose, who was asleep in the chair. Follow me, she mouthed.

We went into the kitchen. She stood on her tiptoes and got a bag of popcorn from a box that was laying on its side. She threw it into the microwave. "Okay, now, what were you saying?"

"Why were you coming on so strong to Medicine Man?"

The first corn popped, I wondered how many watts were Mrs. Channey's microwave. My microwave didn't pop that fast.

"I don't know. I think it has something to do with knowing he has his choice of women."

"You're trying to compete with skeezers?"

She laughed. "I wouldn't expect you to even know that word."

"Emerald is going through her second childhood. She's

hooked on rap videos and Right On magazine. But getting back to you, are you crazy! You can't toy with gangsters. What happens when he's ready for you to pay-up?"

"Hmm, sex with Man."

"What?"

She looked shocked. "Did I say that out loud?"

"Very funny. I'm serious, Jan Channey. I know what you're doing, just like the old days—anything to keep from dealing with the real problems. You can't play with this man. You ought to be ashamed of yourself. By ghetto standards, that child is young enough to be your grandchild."

Jan laughed. "No he's not! And lower your voice, Jose might hear you."

"Why, aren't you finished with him yet?"

She opened the microwave and did something that caused the turntable to start turning again. She was paying way too much attention to that damn popcorn.

"Okay, now, what were you saying?" she asked.

"Why were you coming on so strong to Medicine Man?"

"Man."

"Fine, Man."

A series of kernels popped.

"Ruby, he's twenty years younger than me. Do you remember what twenty-something year olds were like? Just like that Eveready bunny. Being twenty ourselves we didn't know how to appreciate them—I do now."

"Everybody here has warned me about . . ." That triggered that thought again, "Come on," I said, as I pulled her away from the microwave.

"Where are we going?"

"Next door, Mother Stovall is at the root of something, maybe it's this, maybe its insanity, but I've got to find out."

"My popcorn . . ."

"Can wait, let's go." I pulled her to the living room.

She wrote a note to Jose and put it on the TV Guide.

The night air had turned cool. I could smell the bay in the air. It reminded me of how my hometown smells after a good rain.

"Got me out here with no shoes on," Jan mumbled.

I didn't answer. Something was wrong. I felt like we were being watched. "Somebody's watching us, "I whispered.

"That damn Thaddie Stovall, the woman doesn't sleep. She stays up in that window all the time with her phone in her hand set on 911 speed dial."

I looked at the house we were approaching. Maybe she was watching, but the eyes I felt seemed to be on my back. She answered the door before we could ring the doorbell.

"What are you girls doing running around out here this time of night?"

"Mother Stovall, can we talk to you?"

She looked us up and down, like she was trying to decide if we were clean enough to sit on her furniture. "Look at you, running around in stocking feet. Get in here," she said to Jan. I assumed it meant me too. "Give Mother Stovall a hug. You haven't been in my house in a hound's tooth."

That was a new one. I made a mental note to ask my mother how long was a hound's tooth. My mother knows all the old sayings. She just doesn't know the right time to use them. She was subject to say something like, "I haven't seen you in lickety-split."

Jan walked into the old woman's arms and seemed to melt. They rocked like long lost lovers. It was too weird for me.

Weren't these the same people who had been mean-mouthing each other all day? I looked around Mother Stovall's house. It was the "after" picture of Jan's mother's place. It was spotless and it didn't look like an old woman's house. There weren't any dust-catching dollies all over the place and the furniture wasn't covered in plastic. I did notice a small round table by the side window that faced Jan's house, It held a pair of opera glasses and a telephone. There were no signs of her dinner with the insurance man.

"Come sit down," she said to us, her voice cracking like she wanted to cry. I looked at the way she looked at Jan. This woman loved my friend, we had that in common. She had watched her grow

147

up and thought of her as a daughter—a wayward daughter, but her child nonetheless.

"Mother Stovall, Ruby thinks you might know something that will help us."

"Girl, I know that will help the whole human race."

Now that sounded like the woman I'd met earlier, vague and arrogant.

"That's probably true, Mother Stovall, but will you start with me?"

Good one, Jan. They both smiled. Apparently Jan knew how to work little old ladies as well as she worked young gangsters.

"You've got a friend that will come this far to help your sorry ass?"

"Yes, Ma'am. God bless my sorry ass."

"Now you know I don't take with kids cursing around me."

Jan Channey, the fourth decade kid, smiled. "You know somebody is out there trying to kill me, He already shot, maybe killed, one of my friends, thinking she was me.

"No, Lord have mercy. Who'd they get?"

Jan told Mother Stovall the story. While they talked, I looked around the house again. That's when I noticed the bars on the windows. They were white and in a decorative design that Jan would probably be able to name, but bars just the same. Never mind what Emerald might say, I've got a heart and it was breaking for this old lady who had to live alone with bars on her windows and her telephone set on 911 speed dial.

"Looks like your friend here is spaced-out. Is she on that dope?" Mother Stovall asked Jan and my heart stopped breaking.

"I was day-dreaming," I explained.

"Yeah, well . . . "

I never heard what was to come next from Thaddie Stovall's mouth. I heard the sound of breaking glass. Jan hit the floor.

"Get down, Ruby!"

My eyes were on Mother Stovall, her face was red like a bottle of catsup had exploded on her. She was moaning. Jan reached up and

148

pulled her down to the floor with a quick yank. I heard her hit with a thump.

"I didn't hear him drive off like he always does," Jan whispered. Mother Stovall moaned.

I didn't know what to do so I started crawling over to the telephone table. I snatched the cord and pulled the phone towards me, catching it before it hit the floor. I didn't know how to speed dial so I punched in 911.

"Have you been shot?" I heard Jan ask.

"I don't think so, but something hit my face."

Finally, the operator picked up. "Somebody's trying to shoot us!" I screamed into the receiver. The operator made some noises about remaining calm. Boom!

"He's trying to kick in the door," I told the "be calm" woman.

"Let's get out of here," Jan whispered.

"No, he can't kick it in, Do you know how much I paid for that door?"

We didn't hear how much her door cost. A bullet hit the lock. I dropped the phone. If "be calm" didn't have all the information she needed, she wasn't getting it from me. Jan was crawling towards the back and trying to urge Mother Stovall to follow. I dived forward to catch up with them.

"I've got a gun in my bedroom," Mother Stovall argued.

Another shot hit the door. It was followed by the same jiggling at the lock we'd heard before.

"We don't have time for that," Jan whispered.

"You kids go on to the back door. I'm going to get my gun." She didn't wait for Jan's answer, she stood halfway and scooted out of sight. There was another loud kick at the front door.

"Goddamn Oakland police," Jan said, probably reacting to the lack of sirens in the night air,

In the kitchen, Jan stood and ran. I followed. The back door was in an alcove with two other doors. One was the kitchen door and, I imagine, the other led to the laundry room.

"Fu—ck!" Jan said.

I didn't know why until I looked around her. There were three locks on the back door. The top lock had a key in it.

"I hope these bottom ones don't need keys."

She wasn't firing all cylinders to say that, It was plain to see they were the kind of dead-bolts that turned. I was about to ask her why she was being so slow about it, but she answered my questioned unasked.

"If he's given up on the front door, I don't want him to hear us before we get a chance to dash."

"Okay. "

"When we get outside run to the right. He'll expect us to cut left, back to my mother's. There's an opening in the fence in the far right corner. It leads to Mr, Paulk's tool shed. Behind the shed there's an opening that will get us over near the back of the liquor store."

"Got it."

Jan turned the last lock and cracked the door. We held our breath and listened. I didn't hear anything human. I could hear a boom box somewhere nearby and a barking dog, a little too close for comfort—but no big feet. Jan started easing out the door. I couldn't figure out why she didn't just open it and run.

"Open the door," I whispered.

"No, if he's back there he'll see the light and I can't find the switch."

Damn, that Jan Channey could work for the CIA. I eased out behind her. She gently closed the door. I worried about Mother Stovall, but I figured she decided to put her faith in her costly door and hidden gun. I don't blame her. Running through back yards wasn't anything I wanted to do either and I'm at least twenty-five years younger.

We finally heard sirens, still blocks away and not necessarily for us.

"Be careful. No telling what's out here on the ground,"

We heard something fall, something metal--maybe a trash can. Jan shot out towards the back, Her fingernails were digging in the fattest part of my arm, I had no choice but to follow.

TWENTY-ONE
♠

It was like you see in the movies. I heard every beat of my heart pounding in my ears and then the swishing sound of rushing blood. Thaddie Stovall's back yard was even and easy-stepping, but as soon as we wedged our way through the opening in her fence we dropped into a hole.

"Ahh shit!" Jan wailed. "Watch that fucking first step," she warned me, still a few steps behind her. "I twisted my ankle."

I stepped down carefully. I didn't expect Jan's ankle to slow her down, but it seemed to have made her move faster. Her two steps ahead of me was a good five feet by the time I cleared the hole.

"I hope there's no broken glass back here," she said and I remembered she was just wearing socks.

There was a sound like distant thunder and then a loud smashing noise. I pictured him ramming the door with the trash can. If he was at Mother Stovall's door, he was a few feet from us. We froze. We heard him kicking at the door. Persistent mother's son. Jan waited for me to catch up to her. She leaned on my shoulder. "It feel's like it's swelling," she whispered. "Why don't you drop that purse." I shook my head, but I doubt if she saw it. I was sure the purse wasn't interfering with my movement and I was not going to stand in that line to replace my drivers license. We moved slowly, trying very hard not to make any noise, but rustling every thorny bush and crunching every crisp leaf for the next six or seven feet. Jan stopped to listen, forcing me to stop too. Had he heard us?

We heard him near the fence. He'd heard us. He was loud and bold with his . Why wouldn't he be, he had the gun?

We started moving again. I pictured him touching the fence, looking for the opening. There was a smell back there, some small animal had died, I just hoped whatever it was, we wouldn't step on it, "I thought the opening was right here, don't tell me he fixed it."

I wasn't going to be the to tell her. I heard the kicker getting closer. I moved in next to Jan and helped her pat down the wire fence for the opening. A flash of blue light swept the backyard, quickly followed by another. There were no sirens. We kept patting, neither of us confident that help had arrived,

"Here it is," Jan said, a bit too loud.

I could hear the kicker running towards us. He'd found his way through the first fence. We squeezed through an opening large enough for the average five year old. Pop, pop, it sounded like a fire cracker. The bullets must have hit the tool shed. It had to be a small caliber gun, but I wasn't stopping to check. I recognized a smell I associate with my father's hunting rifle.

The police must have heard the gunfire. A white light flooded Mother Stovall's backyard.

"Stop and put down your weapon!" somebody shouted.

He must not have been talking to us, we didn't have weapons. We ran through field that was behind the liquor store.

"Who's that?"

I'd been looking behind us and I didn't see anybody. I turned. A dark figure was running towards us. As soon as I saw him, I saw another man coming towards us from the right side of the field. I recognized this .

We were in the center of a triangle of quickly approaching men. Jan stopped and I bumped into her back. The man to our front left stopped and slowly, deliberately, aimed in our direction, Jan screamed and hit the ground. This time she didn't have to pull or tell me; I'd learned the Oakland Dive.

There was a shot and then two more. I couldn't see what was happening, but I heard somebody fall behind me. I was watching the man who'd been aiming the gun. He turned and ran. The guy to our right screamed out, "You bitch!"

Apparently, he had stopped walking, but now he was coming towards us again. I'd fallen on my purse. I eased out the umbrella.

He didn't seem to be holding anything. I got up on my knees, squatting. I waited. He was focusing on her. Jan was a few feet ahead of me.

"You're going to pay for this," he said, pointing to the fallen man.

"Dante, why are you doing this?"

"Shut- up!"

"When I caught a glimpse of his profile and saw those lips, I knew he was a Luckenbill. He's your brother, isn't he? The you used to go visit in prison at Folsom? He was in the background in that picture that used to be in our living room. He could be alive, you're wasting time," Jan continued.

"I said shut-up! He's dead and it's your fault." He pulled the gun from under his shirt.

I could hear footsteps behind us. There was a lot of them, loud and clumsy. Why haven't they figured out they should drive around the corner, I remembered asking myself.

"Let my friend go, Dante, she ain't got nothing to do with whatever this is." Jan still wasn't begging, but there was less confidence in her voice.

I was ready. I let it drop.

"My purse," I said, not loud enough to frighten him into shooting, but with as much passion as possible.

"Leave it," Dante said.

"Leave it! I've got five hundred dollars cash in there."

I pegged him right. He heard that and took an involuntary step forward. While he was looking down, trying to find my purse in the dark field, I lunged forward with my thumb on the umbrella button.

The police had finally figured out they could get to us by coming around the corner.

We were sitting in a cruiser. The police woman in the front seat had read us our rights, told us not to talk to each other and then ignored us for the next ten or fifteen minutes. Ambulances came for Dante and his brother, but it was obvious, to me, that his brother wasn't going to make it. I counted eleven uniform officers and at least five men in plain clothes. There was a surprising lack of neighborhood gawkers in attendance. Neighborhood folks probably had their own reasons for avoiding the police.

The police were walking, side-by-side through the field for the second time. From the bits and pieces I could hear, they were looking for the gun that shot Dante's brother. I guess they assumed they had all the players and since they had patted us down, another gun had to be somewhere. It's a good thing they didn't ask me anything at that point, I might have told them the truth.

When they finally took us to the police station, we were put in separate rooms and questid. There was a tape player on, but not a reel-to-reel like you see on television sometimes, just a plain old cassette player. I told them everything I knew as it happened,

"Why didn't you tell us about the other man while we were still at the scene?" The asker was a black man, middle-aged and slightly overweight.

"I was told not to talk. And nobody asked me."

He squinted at me, probably trying to figure out if I was smarting-off. He and the other officer, a younger white man, had a side conference. The white man left the room.

"Do you know where you are?" he asked.

It sounded like a trick question so I didn't say anything.

"This is Oakland California, not Gotham City. If we had a man in black who shows up to help people, what makes you think he was waiting for your arrival?"

Yup, trick questions. I still didn't say anything.

"What do you think your friend is going to say?"

"About what?" I asked. He squinted at me even harder this time.

"About-the-man-in-black," he said, like I was a dummy.

"I doubt if she would have been able to see him."

"Does she know him?"

"I didn't get a chance to ask her."

He exhaled loudly.

"Where did the umbrella come from?"

"My purse."

"Before that?"

"Mrs. Channey gave it to me," I repeated for the third time.

"You didn't bring it from Tennessee?"

This time I squinted at him. "No, Mrs. Channey gave it to me," I told him the long version, about the pepper spray and the liposuction. I talked until he made me stop.

"Stop it! Just sit there."

Like I was going to make a run for it?

The white guy returned and they talked. Soon another set of officers came and the four of them asked me the same questions all over again. At least two hours passed before they let me out of the room. I still had to sit at the black detective's desk waiting for another half hour before they brought me my purse. When Jan showed up, she was drinking a diet soda and looking like she'd just gotten up from a nice nap. She was limping on a wrapped ankle and using a cane.

"You okay?" I asked.

"It's not broken, the doctor called it a hairline fracture."

"What doctor?"

"At the hospital. They called Penny's hospital for me too She's going to be all right."

"Who called?"

She looked around and seemed surprised that she was alone. "The cop that was driving me around," she backed up and looked down the hall. "They've been very nice."

Apparently she spotted him because she waved a flirty little wave at somebody I couldn't see. Women that look like Jan Channey have lives so much simpler than the rest of us. "They're not going to charge you with anything," Jan added like it was an after-thought.

"It would have been nice for them to tell me."

It was at least another half hour of sitting around before Jan's "driver" came to tell us we were free to leave. He added that he would see us (looking right in Jan's mouth) home.

I was shocked when we went into Jan's mother's house. Thaddie Stovall was sitting in the living room on the couch next to Glenn. She had a big bandage over her right eye. Mrs. Channey was sitting in her regular chair and the television was off.

"Ruby, call Jose. The poor boy is going crazy with worry," Mrs, Channey said, before anybody had a chance to explain the weird reunion.

I called Jose. He answered on the first ring. He wouldn't let me tell him anything. "I'm on my way," was all he said.

When I got back in the living room, Mother Stovall was helping Jan piece together the story. She told us how she learned that Dante had taken out a policy on Jan and Rasan two years earlier when the Shivs were first messing with them. She figured he didn't think about it again until the house he burned down didn't pay off. With Bay Area home prices being what they are, it was under-insured. It was going to take all the insurance my to rebuild. Glenn had found out, from a Shiv, that Dante had taken out a loan from a neighborhood loan shark; with the understanding that he would pay him back with the home insurance my.

"How is he?" I asked about Dante. It's not that I cared, but I felt I should ask.

"He's in the hospital. They're going to release him to the jail early tomorrow. Pam's at the hospital with him."

Jan and I exchanged glances, Her little sister needed a swift kick in the ass.

Later in the kitchen, Glenn told me and Jan that Man was out of the country. of his boys had contacted Glenn with the message that

Man hopes everything works out for Jan and he expected to see her upon his return. He wished me a safe return to Tennessee.

"How did Man know we were in the field?" I asked Jan later that night. We were at Rasan's other grandparent's house. They offered me a comfortable place to stay until I could leave Oakland. Jan was spending the night with me.

"I don't know. Maybe he had one of his boys following us. Maybe he'd figured out it was Dante and was following him."

"You're going to get with him when he gets back?"

She laughed. "I doubt if he'd come all the way to Tennessee to see somebody's mother."

I didn't ask her if she was serious. I know Jan Channey well enough to know she wouldn't be fooling around with something like that.

"What about Rasan?"

"He's trying to choose between three colleges and they're all in the South. He'll be happy to see me get away from Oakland."

I smiled. What she said wasn't nothing to be sad about.

June 1998

POLKADOTS
Geri Spencer Hunter

0-9639147-5-8
Trade, 5 ½ x 8 ½ $13.00

She sat sipping the wine knowing the young man was staring.

A wickedly seductive mainstream romance that explores the unconventional attraction between a middle-aged black woman and a younger white man.

Set in the world of publishing, **Polkadots** is a vibrant novel with the sass and glamour of WAITING TO EXHALE, written in tight prose comparable to Gloria Naylor and Toni Morrison.

Geri Spencer Hunter is an award winning nonfiction writer. **POLKADOTS** is her first novel. She is a graduate of the University of Iowa.

MURDER BY PROPHECY
Maggie Oliver Anderson

0-9639147-4-X
trade, 5 ½ x 8 ½ $13.00

"Maybe some niggers are just naturally hard to kill!"

He and Martin had received a contract to kill this bitch the first week in December. Since then, five times they'd tried and five times they'd missed

Allison MacWilliams is running out of time. People are dying all around her and now it looks like they're dying *instead* of her. Could an ancient myth really be the key?

Fast paced and deftly plotted, **MURDER BY PROPHECY** is part thriller and part fantasy. It'll leave you breathless and eager for more.

Maggie Oliver Anderson is a prolific writer whose work has appeared in numerous publications. **MURDER BY PROPHECY** in her first thriller.

ORDER FORM

ReGeJe Press, a division of Banks Communications
Invoice Number:
Date:

P.O. Box 293442
Sacramento, CA
(916) 681-5557
Fax: by request

To:

Ship to (if different address):

QTY.	DESCRIPTION	UNIT PRICE	TOTAL
	MAID IN THE SHADE	13.00	
	POLKADOTS	13.00	
	MURDER BY PROPHESY	13.00	

SUBTOTAL	
SALES TAX RATE %	
SALES TAX	
$2.00 FOR THE FIRST BOOK AND 75 CENTS FOR EACH ADDITIONAL BOOK SHIPPING & HANDLING	
TOTAL DUE	

Please add 7.50% for books shipped to California addresses

Make Checks payable to **BANKS COMMUNICATIONS**
THANK YOU FOR YOUR ORDER!